SOULS
TRAPPED IN BODIES

JAMES L. CANNON

Abstract

Join Carter and Warden as they embark on a spiritual quest to discover the anatomy of the human soul and the keys to happiness. In this book, they answer the second of these six epic questions the great Archangel Michael has told them to research and reveal for all humanity:

1. WHAT IS THE MEANING OF HUMAN LIFE ON EARTH?

2. **ARE HUMANS ETERNAL SOULS TRAPPED IN BODIES?**

3. WHAT SPIRITUAL POWERS DO HUMANS POSSESS?

4. WHY IS THERE SUFFERING IN EVERY HUMAN LIFE?

5. IS THERE A WAY MODERN HUMANS SHOULD LIVE?

6. WHAT IS THE MEANING OF DEATH?

Each book in the series involves the answer to one of these questions with which our soul searchers create a modern **non-fiction Handbook of the Soul.** The handbook contains fascinating insights into the human soul and the meaning and purpose of human life.

Thousands of years of global philosophy, theology and science have been examined to find the credible purpose and meaning of human existence. Although the fictional stories surrounding it will entertain you, the handbook's real and rational answers to the timeless questions can help you see the true nature of your soul and the meaning of human life on earth.

Acclaim for the Series

Living as a Modern Soul in a Human Body

An author with an exceptional variety of life experiences has created an exciting series of short books addressing the fundamental questions of human existence.

Viewing life from the unique perspectives of a retired university vice president, a small city mayor, a corporate manager, an undercover intelligence operative, and a decorated military officer, Mr. Cannon provides a concise and thought-provoking account of the essential elements of wisdom necessary for us to thrive and grow.

The six stories, cover life's meaning, the keys to human happiness, and spiritual powers we can all claim, as well as the purpose of virtue, and morality. They also cover ways to encounter God, experience death and how to live well and die well.

The entertaining, six-book series--Living as a Modern Soul in a Human Body--was created to pass a very practical and valuable body of moral, ethical and spiritual knowledge to future generations. However, I heartily recommend the series as a great and easy read for anyone interested in becoming all they can be while on this Earth.

Jerry L. Beasley
President Emeritus
Concord University

Table of Contents

Book 2

SOULS TRAPPED IN BODIES

Series

The six books included in the serial series *Living as a Modern Soul in a Human Body* are best read in the following order:

Book 1: *The Meaning of Life*

Book 2: *Souls Trapped in Bodies*

Book 3: *Human Spiritual Powers*

Book 4: *Why Human Suffering*

Book 5: *A Soul's Code of Conduct*

Book 6: *The Meaning of Death*

SOULS TRAPPED IN BODIES

Book 2 in the Series

Living as a
Modern Soul in a Human Body

JAMES L. CANNON

Printed in the United States of America

ISBN-13:978-0-9968528-3-8

This book is dedicated with love to my wife
Brenda M. Cannon

Scriptural verses from KJV

On the cover:
Renaissance genius Leonardo da Vinci's famous 1490 drawing the Vitruvian Man (soul and apron added). With the body as the temple of the soul, da Vinci shows that there is great harmony in the symmetrical relation of the human body's parts to the whole. The body's proportions extend to the circumference of a perfect circle with its center at the navel and a perfect square when centered at the groin.

Introduction

This is the 2nd book in the six-book serial set **Living as a Modern Soul in a Human Body**. In Book 2, *Souls Trapped in Human Bodies*, we discuss the status of human souls on Earth and the soul's anatomy, nature and faculties. We will cover spiritual character and reasons for our earthly journeys. In addition, we will talk about improving our souls, two measures of human happiness, the secrets to joy and happiness and happiness at work.

The books in this series use an ongoing adventure story to convey vital spiritual truths. Those truths are outlined in the Handbook of the Soul section of each chapter, which I hope will give you a spiritual lift.

For clarity, **important points and concepts** are **repeated** and **expanded** from chapter to chapter. The spiritual intelligence in the Handbook of the Soul is presented in a bulleted outline format of thought-sized bites for easier, reading. The glossary of significant terms as used in this series is located at the end of Book 1. The bibliography can be found at the back of books 1 and 6.

While acknowledging many and varied sources of information, it is the author who ultimately responsible for the content, and it is my earnest hope that these pages will help make life a little more meaningful for those whose eyes may chance upon them.

James L. Cannon
Soulsline9@gmail.com
31 January 2020

"The soul is the connecting link between God and man..."
...Van Brunt Wyckoff

Chapter 1

<u>**Anatomy of the Soul I**</u>

P eering through a dirty, weed covered basement window in the back of a funeral home during a thunderstorm, Warden spies Carter gagged and tied in a bed suspended from two large weighing scales in the basement with a madman about to kill him.

That morning Warden had awakened to find Carter missing. "Where could he be?" thought Warden. "He was here last night talking to a Mr. MacDougall about weighing the soul." Asking around Athens, he found out that MacDougall was the eccentric owner of a funeral home who had been trying to find a dying person to weigh to see if their weight changed when the soul departed at the moment of death.

By noon Warden, really worried, caught a ride to the MacDougall's funeral home to look around. It was closed and no one answered the door. He sensed Carter was near and in trouble, so despite the pouring rain, he snooped around until he found the basement window in the back of the building.

Acting quickly Warden throws a brick sized rock through the window causing MacDougall to drop a large knife and flee. Warden kicks the remaining glass out and slides down into the basement to free Carter. They quickly exit the building and race back to the Athens Park.

On the way, Carter says, "Last night, MacDougall told me he had a way to weigh the human soul and asked if I would like to see him do so."

"Warden, I should have awakened you to let you know I was going," said Carter, "but it was late, you were asleep and MacDougall just seemed like a crackpot. But you know I had to check it out, so I went with him to his funeral home. Little did I know mine was the soul to be weighed. Upon arrival I was knocked out from behind and awakened tied in the bed. Thank goodness you showed up when you did and thanks for saving my hide."

Hello to our readers, I'm Carter. As you may know, my cousin Warden and I are spiritual pilgrims on a quest to find the answers to six age-old questions about the human Soul. In Book 1, we discovered the meaning of life and, we are now on an expedition to discover the answer to the second great inquiry of our spiritual quest:

ARE HUMAN BEINGS ETERNAL SOULS TRAPPED IN BODIES?

We are in the third evening of our stay in the tree-lined Athens Town Park to hear from an enlightened medical doctor, pastor and former army chaplain, Dr. M. A. Moses. It is a warm summer evening, with a light breeze, and the park is full of people hoping to hear the doctor speak. A police canine unit is in attendance due to an attack yesterday by APOLLYON a violent God hating network of radical socialist political extremists who try to stir up racial division and rough up Dr. Moses whenever they can find him.

The doctor is now greeting people and shaking hands as is his custom. He has moved to the park gazebo, and is telling us he is going to speak about the human soul, its anatomy and the function and purpose of each essential feature. So far, there is no sign of APOLLYON. Let us listen carefully to what he says as we take notes for our Handbook of the Soul.

> "The only person you are destined to become
> is the person you decide to be."
> ... *Ralph Waldo Emerson*

Handbook of the Soul

Anatomy of the Soul I

"As a medical doctor it is natural that I should teach anatomy," said Doctor Moses, and added, "As a humble seeker of spiritual truth, I will also share what I have learned of the purpose and function of each aspect of the human soul and identify some of its properties."

With a mellow voice, the enlightened physician said, "It is important to realize that we are majestic, transcendent, eternal souls and spirits that are designed to grow through life's challenges."

Your Soul. Have you ever wondered exactly what a soul is? We talk and read about it a little, but do you actually know the nature of your soul; what it does and who it is? People often think of it like a pilot light burning inside themselves or a spark from the firestorm of God. Maybe a piece of golden clay or dental mold, that collects the sum of a person's **experiences**--*endless impressions of happiness, worry, fear, love and all the emotions we've ever known and all the* **choices** *we ever made.*

I. Preview

The human soul is composed of Mental States, Faculties, Capacities and Aspects of Spiritual Character. Also, our Consciousness, Transcendence and Conscience are among many properties of the soul. Spiritual character is an eternal work in progress that helps shape your daily moral and ethical choices, and is itself shaped by those same choices.

**Feed your faith (by thinking about it),
and your fears (by not thinking about them) will starve to death.**

II. Introduction

The human soul does not develop naturally from genetic material like the physical body. Instead, after conception, God imparts a soul to every embryo able to receive it.[1] Our human souls, he added, are individual sparks of Divine energy.

1. *Souls are immaterial entities consisting of mental properties that enable mental events including perceptions, sensations, capacities for imaginings, memories and hopes, thoughts, and feelings, dreams, desires, beliefs and more.[2]*

2. *The soul may well be embodied sooner, but based on the development of a brain sufficient to support its operations, it begins to function about twenty weeks after conception. [3]*

We Are Souls *- Human scriptural traditions say money, success and pleasure bring no lasting satisfaction but only a desire for more of the same. This is because one of life's greatest truths is that we are not just bodies with brains, we are souls with bodies and brains. A human being is a soul – a non-physical entity, a life principle, a ground of consciousness and locus of personal identity-- fully inhabiting a body.*

As much as the body needs food, water and shelter, the soul has needs like the following:

- *Values and Beliefs as Guidelines for Living and Maturing*

- *Meaning, Purpose and Challenges for Development*

- *Recognition of the Soul's Personal Character and Identity*

- *Love and a Connection to Others*

- *Communion with Divinity*

"If we ignore this truth -- if we feed our bodies but starve our souls -- we will be incomplete and unfulfilled, and we will find ourselves weak and unprepared for life's inevitable trials. Sooner or later the storms of life will overwhelm us, and we will discover that we have built our lives on foundations of sand." [4]

III. Nature of the Soul

The spirit and soul are closely related, and like wind and gravity, they are invisible forces of great power.

1. *The soul is a **unified consciousness**[5] that combines perceptions and experiences and directs its body. We know this because as souls we have direct first-person introspective awareness allowing us to experience our own consciousness.*

   A third-person view of things is based on someone else's view of what pain or pleasure you are feeling based on what they might observe of your reaction. It invariably involves a lot of guesswork on their part as to the exact nature and intensity of your feelings.

   On the other hand, the first-person point of view is based on your own personal view of how you are feeling based on your immediate experience and insight. Therefore, it is much more accurate with no need for guesswork. It provides us with direct and unique awareness of our own pleasures and pains as well as our thoughts, choices, hopes, fears and the other functions of our souls.[6]

   Most of us understand that our soul is that to which our pure mental properties belong. And that we are conscious, aware, thinking, feeling and acting beings, with a lifetime of direct first-person experience with the functioning of our own souls.[7]

   Science has found no physical organ that originates our first-person mental functions. Although our brain is necessary to convey external sensations to us and to transmit intentions into physical actions through its neurons, it does not originate conscious activity.

2. *The soul has a **structure of interconnected beliefs and desires**, integrated and mutually supporting to a greater or lesser degree. This belief-desire set influences a person's behavior in a way that often involves a tradeoff between what he believes is right verses what he desires to do.[8]*

> **"The real measure of your wealth is how much you'd be worth**
> **if you lost all your money."**
> *... Bernard Meltzer*

Desire is said to be like a stream which carries us onward unless we swim against it. And swimming against it requires effort.[9]

People will **resist a desire only** if they believe there is good reason for doing so. Good reasons for resisting a desire may be based on personal beliefs and values or on practical reasons like possible unfavorable consequences of yielding to the desire. Otherwise, people usually will follow their desires whatever they may be.[10]

Human beings may not always be able to control which desires come upon them; however, they can determine which of those they yield to and act upon.

For example, if you have a firm belief that you need to avoid overeating and gluttony you are more likely to control your desire for too much dessert. Whereas, if you also have some degree of conflicting belief that you only live once and you should therefore indulge yourself, then your desire for dessert may be a little more difficult to control. Your activity will be governed ultimately by the combined impact of related values, beliefs, desires and will power.

Education can instill in people a broader understanding of the long-term benefits of not always indulging in their immediate short-term desires. For example, learning how much saving and investing a part of your earnings for future prosperity will benefit you instead of spending it all, will add to your belief-desire set and may help you control your spending.

The extent to which new desires and beliefs are recognized depends, **in part,** on their compatibility with your soul's existing central belief-desire set, which is usually subject only to gradual change.[11]

People are not necessarily aware of all their beliefs and desires. When a person is consciously aware of her beliefs and desires, she will be more aware of some than others depending on the issues currently on her mind with awareness also being a matter of degree.[12]

3. The better **integrated and consistent** the soul's spiritual **character,** the firmer its structure and the less conflict will ensue between belief and desire. With consistent character, each belief and desire is

supported with meaning and justification by many other similar beliefs and desires.[13]

For instance, you might believe honesty requires that you return a wallet full of money you found even though you really need and desire the cash. Thus, the belief in honesty is in conflict with the desire for the money. Hopefully, a uniformly virtuous, well integrated spiritual character will give rise to an act of will to motivate the money's return.

4. *We know from our own first-person experience that we can effortlessly will our bodies to movement. The soul and its spirit relate to our physical beings through **quantum neural interaction**. Mental events in our soul's mind (generated by an act of will) create purposeful intentions that trigger quantum level physical events in our brains that stimulate our nervous systems to cause our muscles to move in the ways intended.*

5. *It has been said that the developing human body is a physical expression of the soul within.[14] that the spirit/soul have a form and facial features similar to the body they inhabit, retaining those features and its sensory functions when departing at death.[15]*

We are unified and complicated beings with various faculties and abundant capacities that interact and affect one another. The condition of the body can affect faculties and states of the soul and their conditions affect the body because the body and soul interact closely and depend one on another.[16]

A soul can affect the external world around it through its brain and body, and the soul can be affected through its body and brain or by divine intervention.

6. *Being of divine origin, souls have the property of **transcendence** making them undying or immortal thus allowing them to move beyond the physical reality of this dimension once disengaged from this physical body at its death. It may be sustainable by Divinity for an unknown period of time before requiring re-embodiment.*

7. *The soul is eternal. One way or another at the end of a thousand ages you will still exist. The only question is where?[17]*

8. *The immaterial soul fully occupies the body it animates and is **located** in the same space but in a different way. Being non-physical in nature, the soul extends to all points in the body without being spatially located anywhere within it.[18] The soul in its ethereal entirety is simultaneously present at all locations within its body.[19] Some believe it resides in the blood.*

Philosopher Richard Swinburne explains that the soul is like a light bulb, and the brain is like an electric light socket. If you plug the bulb into the socket and turn the power on, the light will shine. If the socket is damaged or the power turned off, the light will not shine. So too, the soul will function (have a mental life) if it is plugged into a functioning brain. Destroy the brain or cut off the nutriment supplied by the blood and the soul will cease to function yet may remain intact like the lightbulb.[20]

Most brain disease, injury, surgery and drugs affect human capacity for acting more than they affect character which involves values, virtue and beliefs found in the depths of the soul. [21]

Some scientists, philosophers and mystics have speculated that the soul's point of entry into and exit from the body could be the pineal gland, a tiny organ at the center of our brains.[22] The pineal gland secretes the so-called "spirit molecule" DMT that may facilitate the entry and exit of the human life force.[23]

The soul is said to be of a spiritually uniform substance, but the nature of its properties including powers, mental states, faculties and capacities is considered to be very complex. In the soul, countless qualities can be found in various states and each in varying degree.[24]

Biologists tell us that every part of our bodies down to the smallest molecule, is replaced several times in our lifetimes. So, who am I if I am constantly changing physically, with the specific set of particles that now comprise my body and brain being completely different from the atoms and molecules that I was comprised of some time ago?

Most of our cells are turned over in a matter of weeks and even our neurons change all of their constituent molecules within a month. The actin filaments in nerve cell dendrites are replaced every 40 seconds. The proteins that power the synapses between our nerve cells are replaced about every hour.

In short, my body is made up of a completely different set of stuff than it was a year ago, and all that persists is the pattern of organization of that stuff.[25]

Yet, despite being physically different, I persist in my original conscious identity, remaining the same person with the same memories and relationships that I have had all along. That continuity of identity with all its properties and associations is a function of my soul.

IV. Properties of the Soul

Lacking perceptible physical mass, souls are weightless. Among the properties of the soul are its Powers, Mental States and Capacities grouped as Faculties. Powers may be exercised such as the powers to think, choose and forgive while capacities may be actualized as in believing, desiring, experiencing and so on.[26]

There are at least five potential mental states of the soul listed below:[27,28]

1. **Sensation** - *A conscious awareness in the mind of sensory perception*

2. **Thought** - *A mental construct that often could be expressed as a complete sentence and exists only while it is being thought.*

3. **Belief** - *A soul's views of reality including the values it believes in*

4. **Desire** - *An inclination to do, have, or experience things*

5. **Act of Will** - *A free choice, an act of power or an initiation of activity*

Desires, and beliefs can be continuing mental states; sensations thoughts and acts of will are each conscious episodes of some limited duration.[29]

Our character, including what we think is worthwhile, how we naturally direct our lives and how we are inclined to cope with our sufferings, successes and desires is a central element of our belief-desire set. Our character doesn't always determine our choices, but it does make certain choices more likely and others less likely.[30]

In addition to its mental states, the adult soul has a great many capacities such as the capacity to love, think or imagine. Similar capacities are grouped together into Faculties. A Faculty of the Soul is an area of the soul containing a natural family of related capacities.[31]

Faculties of the Human Spirit and Soul:

*1. **Spirit**: The faculty through which a person relates to God and the repository of his or her character. Distinct from the soul.*

*2. **Mind**: That faculty of the soul that contains thoughts and beliefs along with the relevant abilities to form them. It includes capacities to realize senses of sight, taste, hearing, touch and smell and many other mental capacities including memory.*

*3. **Will**: A faculty of the soul that contains our ability to choose*

*4. **Emotion**: One's faculty to experience fear, love etc.*

Each Faculty of the human soul is discussed in more detail on the following pages in terms of its function and purpose.[32]

Faculties and Properties of the Human Soul
Schematic Diagram

1. *The Human Spirit*

The first faculty of our soul is our human spirit, which is the eternal life force that in the earthly realm connects us to the Divine. Our spirit has been called the conscious force that is life itself.

In human experience, the spirit and soul are often considered as one in the same. They are frequently used interchangeably with both being referenced as either spirit or soul or frequently simply as heart.

For simplicity in this book series, we will consider the spirit as a faculty of the soul, but the **foremost** part of the soul.

Although invisible to the physical senses, our spirit is the individual, permanent essence of our being. Without a living spirit, our-connection to God and eternity ends.

- The spirit within the human soul, sustains our human **consciousness** which includes self-awareness plus other aspects of perception including time.[33]

- It is written that our spirits are a separate substance from our bodies created directly by God that only He can destroy.

- However, we can purify or corrupt the **character** of our spirits in the human dimension of existence.

Our **conscience** is a voice of our spirit and one means through which God can speak to us. It also serves to reminds us that we should behave according to what we believe is right and wrong. However, it does not teach us what is right or wrong. Therefore, it could be corrupted if we have been taught error and believe untruth.

A. *Purpose* - The purpose of your spirit is to provide your sustaining life force. A strong spirit keeps at bay the demoralizing influence of fear and worry.

According to Professor Reinhold Niebuhr, American theologian and ethicist, the human spirit in its depth and height reaches into eternity[34]

B. *Function* - Your spirit functions as the source of your **conscious self-awareness, moral character** and **conscience** and your powers of **intuition, insight, creativity** and **inspiration.**

The content of your spiritual character includes your virtues and vices,[35] which are woven into much of what you say and do. Your personal attitude and personality reflect the developmental stages of your spirit and its interaction with the chemical elements of your earthbound human body.

Character is the inner core of being and the qualities of the spirit that help make people who they are. It is the distinguishing characteristic of your eternal identity. On Earth, your spiritual character is known as your **human moral** and **ethical character.**

Character affects behavior just as behavior demonstrates character. Character informs life and life **forms** character through temptation and stress, failure and success.

Aspects of personality can be genetic, but character is neither inherited nor automatic; it must be formed and developed, and it can develop evil qualities as well as good ones with either virtue or vice.[36]

<u>**Virtuous Character**</u> In the home, good character is love and kindness; in business, it is honesty; in society, it is courtesy; in work, it is dedication; in play, it is fairness.

Virtuous character toward the fortunate is congratulations; toward the weak, it is help; toward the wicked, it is resistance; toward the penitent, it is forgiveness; and toward God, it is reverence and love.

Character is the driving force and evolving compass of the spiritual transformation that can take you from **what you are** to the **very best** that **you can become.** Your character is an eternal work in progress that helps shape your daily moral and ethical choices, and is itself **shaped by** those same choices.

<u>**Improve Your Character**</u> - In this life, each soul has the opportunity to form good character with the day-to-day decisions it makes that incorporate the highest ideals of human excellence such as selflessness, courage, self-control, faith, hope and love.

Be like melting snow; wash yourself of yourself
...Jalāl al-Dīn Rūmī

Every Choice - *As author and Professor C.S. Lewis noted, "**Every time you make a moral or ethical choice** you are turning the central part of you, the part that chooses, into something a little different than what it was before."*

Each day our character is increasingly formed, and with each choice we make, we move either toward or away from God. As the direction of our character emerges, certain choices become easier but others increasingly unlikely.[37] For example, the longer one lives in opposition to God the harder it becomes to turn toward God due, perhaps, to a hardening of the attitudes.

*Taking your life as a whole, with all your thousands of moral choices, **you are slowly refining** your spiritual self into a **more heavenly** creature or a **more hellish** creature; a more noble or less noble being; a more virtuous soul or a less virtuous soul.*

- *Each choice you make eventually moves you a little closer to the unselfish joy and peace of heaven or a little closer to the madness and horror of further selfishness and separation from Divinity.*

- *Every time you shed a bit of your selfishness by giving up something you prefer or desire, in favor of someone else, your spirit and soul gain a bit of wisdom and grace in its place.*

- *Wisdom and goodness cannot be bought with money; only at the cost of selfishness and vice can they be purchased.*

- *You have, in life, the ongoing choice and opportunity to make yourself into a wise and truth-loving being or not.*

Spiritual Strength - *Your spiritual strength and wisdom are improved as you increase your ability to **control** and **eliminate undisciplined, negative** and **corrupt forces** within your character such as:*

- *Bad Temper*
- *Selfishness*
- *Fear*
- *Impatience*

Positive Qualities - *Spiritual strength is further advanced by **fully developing the positive qualities** of your character such as:*

- *Joy*
- *Generosity*
- *Honor*
- *Kindness*

Our spirits are very much a part of our ongoing daily existence helping shape our thoughts and emotions.

- *Our **conduct** and the **relationships** of our lives are affected by our spirits just as our spirits are affected by them.*

- *Being involved in too much negativity, moral misconduct and strife depletes the positive energy of our spirits often leading to physical illness and possibly an early demise.*

- *The many trials, temptations, victories and defeats of human life are only opportunities to practice overcoming **negative spiritual force** with **positive spiritual force**.*

- *We must **learn to manage** fear with faith, success with humility, failure with courage and depression with joy.*

- *Likewise, we should learn to manage strife with harmony, selfishness with concern for others and temptation with discipline and self-control.*

Courage, Commitment and Desire - *Overcoming **negative spiritual force** with **positive spiritual force** can be far from easy, and it requires a great deal of courage, commitment and desire. However, it can lead to a life so much better than the selfish, negative, fearful and critical existence in which so many are now immersed.*

- *Eventually, crises of life situations test our faith.*

The only thing on earth that can fashion itself by itself is a human soul.
...Author Austin O'Malley in Keystones of Thought

- *We can become absorbed in the selfish or negative strife of life to the extent that it is affecting our attitude and robbing our spiritual vitality.*

- *At times, we may need to pull back, **radically change our situation** to restore the positive energy of our spirit.*

According to many sacred texts, to heal from the misdirection of our spirits, we must be willing to release the past and cleanse our spirit through confession in prayer, forgiveness and repentance (change). Doing so may be a continuous process throughout our existence.

Benefits *– A powerful spirit enables humans to do the following:*

- *Perceive and receive more Divine guidance*

- *Overcome more difficulty and temptation, live more virtuously in God's grace and become more compatible with Divinity*

- *Provide more assistance to others*

In his book The Measure of a Man Twenty Attributes of a Godly Man,[38] Gene Getz makes the following points regarding the process of spiritual conversion:

1. *Believing in God involves an act of will. We can choose to turn our spirit to draw upon God's strength and power to live a holy and righteous life. Becoming transformed with righteousness and faith brings peace with God, but it's a lifelong process.*

2. *The process of becoming holy in spirit, soul and body is uniquely linked with how we use our minds, which are renewed in the process of spiritual conversion. Scriptures say not to be conformed to this world but to be transformed by the renewing of your mind.*

3. *The evidence of a gradual spiritual conversion to holiness is to be seen in the change of a person's behavior with less immorality, impurity, sensuality, dissensions, strife, jealously, anger, disputes, envying, drunkenness and, carousing; and more love, joy, peace,*

patience, kindness, goodness, faithfulness, gentleness and self-control.

Concluding his talk Dr. Moses says he will continue the description of the human soul tomorrow with the soul's second faculty the mind.

Warden and Carter catch him before he leaves and ask if he ever heard of a method of weighing the soul, and they go on to explain what MacDougall had tried to do to Carter.

Most interesting, says the doctor, because as it happens in 1907, a Doctor Duncan MacDougall of Haverhill, Massachusetts did exactly what this MacDougall tried to do with Carter but without murdering the patients. In 1907, he managed six times to get a dying patient onto a bed hanging from a set of sensitive weighing scales. He reported that in only four of the six cases was he able to get proper measurements at the time of death.

Accounts of MacDougal's experiments were published In March 1907 in the journal American Medicine and the New York Times Newspaper. The results of his four measurements varied and he acknowledged that many such tests with more consistent results would have to be conducted before any valid conclusions could be drawn. However, based on his experiments he estimated the weight of the human soul to be about 21 grams.

In 1911, the New York Times reported in a front-page story that he had moved on to trying to get photographs of the soul by experimenting with X rays. There has been no confirmation that the soul has any mass or weight at all and no success with X ray photography. Dr. MacDougal died in 1920.

Dr. Moses went on to suggest that they report the incident at the funeral home to the police.

Why, asks Warden, do you suppose we have to die to get into heaven? I mean why couldn't we just be born into heaven to start with?

Ordinary riches can be stolen; real riches cannot. In your soul are infinitely precious things that cannot be taken from you.
...Playwright Oscar Wilde

Well, as I understand it, responds the good doctor, we couldn't have been born into heaven to start with because admission to heaven involves **a choice each soul has to make.** To qualify for heaven, you must **choose** to be **spiritually reborn** with a sincere desire to become **holy enough** to survive the journey and prosper in heaven.

You must have a desire sincere enough to overcome human pride and accept through faith and humility that you **need** the saving mercy, grace and love of God. A love expressed in the sacrifice of his only Son to purchase for you a one-way ticket into the heavenly realm. A ticket you can see and hold only with faith, love, gratitude, hope and humility (holiness).

What if a person wins a one hundred-million-dollar lottery, but is too drunk or stoned to realize they won? They would miss out on their reward due to the flaws in their own character.

In a more spiritual context, you could have a free, all-expense paid trip to heaven, but if, when it's time to go, you are so involved in carnal pleasure, selfishness, greed or materialism that you cannot see your ticket or hear the boarding call, you will miss the flight due to the flaws in your own character. We must clean ourselves up spiritually now, because no one knows the date or the time of his or her flight.

We are strangers on earth; our real home lies in heaven where God dwells. This body was created from the earth, but the soul and spirit were created for eternity. The present body returns to earth, but the righteous souls and spirits return to God who gave them life. (Eccl. 12:6)

This concludes Anatomy of the Soul I. The description of the soul's faculties continues in the next chapter, Anatomy of the Soul II, where we will begin with the human soul's second faculty the Mind.

...And may your whole spirit, soul and body be preserved blameless[39]...

---

[1] Richard Swinburne, The Evolution of the Soul, NY, Oxford U. Press, 2007, p199
[2] Ibid p.17, 333
[3] Ibid p.179
[4] Billy Graham, Nearing Home, Thomas Nelson, p.134

---

[5] S. Goetz & C. Taliaferro, A Brief History of the Soul, Wiley Blackwell, Oxford, p.18

[6] Baker, Goetz et al, The Soul Hypothesis, NY, Bloomsbury, 2013 p.22

[7] Ibid p.26

[8] Richard Swinburne, The Evolution of the Soul, NY, Oxford U. Press, 2007, p.263,295

[9] Ibid p.259

[10] Ibid p.260

[11] Ibid p.278

[12] Ibid pp. 293, 295

[13] Ibid p.296

[14] S. Goetz & C. Taliaferro, A Brief History of the Soul, Wiley Blackwell, Oxford, p.79

[15] Perry Stone, Secrets of the Third Heaven, Voice of Evangelism Ministries, Cleveland, TN p.109,110.

[16] Habermas, Gary, Beyond Death, Wipf and Stock, Eugene, 2004, p.74

[17] Cahn, Jonathan, The Harbinger, Front Line, Lake Mary, FL, 2011, p. 230

[18] Habermas, Gary, Beyond Death, Wipf and Stock, Eugene, 2004, p.68

[19] S. Goetz & C. Taliaferro, A Brief History of the Soul, Wiley Blackwell, Oxford, p.44

[20] Richard Swinburne, The Evolution of the Soul, NY, Oxford Univ. Press, 2007, p.312

[21] Ibid p. 263, 276

[22] Rick J. Strassman M.D., DMT the Spirit Molecule, Park St. Press Rochester, VT, 2001, p.61

[23] Ibid, p.68

[24] S. Goetz & C. Taliaferro, A Brief History of the Soul, Wiley Blackwell, Oxford, p.45

[25] Ray Kurzweil, The Singularity is Near, Penguin Books, NY, 2005, p.383

[26] S. Goetz & C. Taliaferro, A Brief History of the Soul, Wiley Blackwell, Oxford, p.123

[27] Richard Swinburne, The Evolution of the Soul, NY, Oxford Univ. Press, 2007, p.333

[28] Gary Habermas, Beyond Death, Wipf and Stock, Eugene, 2004, p.69

[29] Richard Swinburne, The Evolution of the Soul, NY, Oxford Univ. Press, 2007, p.18

[30] Ibid p.269

[31] Gary Habermas, Beyond Death, Wipf and Stock, Eugene, 2004, p.73

[32] J.P. Moreland, The Soul: How We Know It's Real: Chicago: Moody, 2014, p.124-125

[33] Prof. Sean Carroll, Time: Mystery of Physics, Teaching Co., Course PC1257 p.109

[34] David Brooks, The Road to Character, Random House, NY, New York ,2015 p.196

[35] Book 5 of this series lists 37 traits of virtue or vice that comprise spiritual character.

[36] Os Guinness, Character Counts, Baker Books, Grand Rapids MI, p.12 &13

[37] J.P. Moreland., The Soul: How We Know It's Real: Chicago: Moody, 2014, p.143

[38] Gene Getz, The Measure of a Man, Revell, Grand Rapids, 2016, p.237-239

[39] 1st Thessalonians 5:23

What lies behind us and what lies ahead of us are tiny matters compared to what lies within us.
...Henry Stanley Haskins

Chapter 2

<u>Anatomy of the Soul II</u>

Handbook of the Soul

This chapter continues the description of the Faculties of the human soul, each of which is a grouping of similar Capacities. The first Faculty of your soul, covered in the previous chapter, is your Spirit with your spiritual character, which is the core of your being. The second Faculty of your soul is your mind.

2. <u>The Human Mind</u>

Your immortal mind is the second faculty of your soul. It is the thinking and memory component of your being, also providing the ability to consider alternatives; reality or future possibilities.

- *While on earth in human form, the mind works **through** the physical brain to operate the human body.*

- *The human brain consists of about 100 billion neurons, and damage to the brain can affect the mind's operation.*

- *Your mind is known as the battlefield for control of your soul, because it is in your thinking that the battles between virtue and vice (corruption) are fought. It is your thoughts, properly managed, that can give you control of your life.*

- *It is estimated that most humans have thousands of thoughts a day. How many of those thoughts are you controlling, and how many are controlling you?*

A. *<u>Function</u> - Your mind functions as your central control interface with the rest of your being.*

The renewing of your mind is an ongoing process of becoming more and more compatible with Divinity.

- *Thoughts projected in your mind, usually through your will, move your body to specific action, and affect all aspects of your being.*

- *Ideas can emerge through your mind, and it gives you the power to compute information, to calculate logically and to set the course of your existence every day.*

- *Your mind, in conjunction with your brain, also provides your short and long-term memory functions.*

- *Your mind uses the data from your sensory organs and reason to provide its best estimate and understanding of the reality around you and the situations you deal with each day.*

- *Through experience and education, your mind should develop the virtue of practical wisdom or prudence to help you discern the best course of action in any given circumstance.*

Reason is a purely abstract quality that comes midway between the animal and divine consciousness in man.

- *If properly employed, reason leads from the darkness of spiritual ignorance to the light of divine consciousness.*

- *A fuller development of reason leads away from our selfish natures and can ultimately align our souls more closely with God.*

B. Purpose - *The purpose of your human mind is to support the thought process that operates your being.*

Your mind is subject to self-control, control by your body or external forces. Through growth and development, your spirit should gain and maintain control of your mind and through it your entire being.

*One of the most profound truths pertaining to your soul is that you can be the **master of your thinking** and thereby the architect of your character and, to **some extent**, an engineer of your own destiny!*

"Some bright morning when this life is over, I'll fly away."
"When I die, Hallelujah, by and by, I'll fly away."
...Gospel spiritual [1]

3. <u>Human Will</u>

*The third faculty of your Soul is your human Will. It contains the capacities for will power, personal drive and **self-determination**. You are equipped with a "free will" that allows you to function independently of God and the other beings with you here on earth.*

- *Your will can be used to manage the thoughts in your mind.*

- *The functional center of your will is between the energies of your mind and the energies of your emotions. In most people, one of these energies has more influence.*

- *The seat of the will, which is to say a concentration of the will's energy, seems to be in the brain. It is not, however, a physical organ, but more a concentrated force of very personal energy.*

Souls cause events to occur in the physical world by making choices.[2] Your free will allows you the choice to engage in all manner of good or evil behavior. Your will has a natural, if selfish, bias in favor of whatever your mind thinks will make you happy.

*Your will should also have a countervailing concern for the moral virtue of justice that should be keeping you from hurting other people in the pursuit of your own happiness. It bears repeating that with **will power** you can **control** your **thinking and your actions**!*

Wisdom *- Learning to nurture and honor your sense of justice and fairness in the application of your will power is a key determinate of your spiritual development. It gives you the power to choose restraint and avoid selfishness. The process of learning to manage your choices is called wisdom.*

According to philosopher James Allen, "The essential difference between a wise person and a fool is that the wise control their thinking; but the fools are controlled by theirs."

A. Function *- Your will has the power to direct thought in your mind.*

- *Your will should be under the control of your spirit; however, a weak will can be overridden and redirected by your mind, body or external forces.*

- *Your will is like spiritual muscle, and it responds well to exercise, so use it often.*

__B. Purpose__ - Your will is a focal point of spiritual force designed to channel your human power into the motivation, direction and activity of your own choosing. Managing our power of choice is a sacred contract that we are here to fulfill. It begins with choosing what the nature of our thoughts and attitudes will be.[3]

As beings of free will, we even have the option of rejecting a relationship with God or freely choosing to establish one on faith. Unfortunately, we cannot choose to undo choices already made in the past; we can only make better choices going forward.

Lacking willpower and self-control, millions of people consider themselves as mere putty in the hands of fate. When, in fact, as Sir Francis Bacon wrote, "Chiefly the mold of a man's fortune is in his own hands."

__Open Gates__ - Professor of theology, C.S. Lewis, suggests that heaven's gates are always open and that we are never prevented from entering by any power or will but our own.[4]

- *It has been said that __self-control__ is the __door to heaven__. It has no substitute; nothing can take the place of self-control.*

- *There is no power in the universe that can do for humans that which they, sooner or later, must do for themselves by entering the practice of self-control.[5]*

4. __Human Emotions__

Finally, the fourth faculty of your soul includes your emotional capacities, which are the passions of your soul, establishing the feelings in your consciousness that collectively create changing human moods.

Your emotions interface directly with the mental and physical aspects of your being. They affect and are affected by electro-chemical activity in certain neural networks of your brain and by some of the hormonal aspects of your physical body.

Strength is not of physical capacity, but from an indomitable will.
...Indian Leader Mohandas K. Gandhi

A. Function - *Emotions function as largely non-intellectual but complex responses to internal and external stimulus.*

- *Emotions infuse your being with feeling and are sometimes rational and sometimes irrational. The limbic system in the brain distributes the physical impact of emotional activity in the soul.*

- *Most people have the capacities to experience ten universal or primary human emotions. Among these are anger, fear, love, compassion, pride, envy, joy, jealousy, vengeance and sadness.*

Panic and Horror - *The basic emotions exist in numerous variations and combinations. For instance, variations on fear include panic, anxiety and horror.*

- *Your emotions are in a state of continuous adjustment and response to changing stimulus.*

- *The overall balance or state of your emotions at any given time establishes your existing "mood."*

B. Purpose - *Your emotions provide a vast multi-dimensional aspect of your living experience, enriching and amplifying in your soul the effect of activity and stimulus.*

- *Harnessing your emotions serves as part of the process of gaining wisdom and spiritual character development.*

- *As your spiritual control grows, the nature of your predominate emotions can become more positive with more happiness, peace and harmony and less anger, jealousy or fear. This process is evident as babies mature into children and then to adults, they gain more control over their emotions.*

- *Likewise, as you progress through your adult life, you should continue to gain control over your emotions especially those that can be negative and destructive.*

__Emotional Power__ - Channel the power of your emotions to reinforce the positive values in your consciousness.

- *Grip the positive aspirations of your soul (goodness, divine love, harmony, belief in yourself and in your future) and flood them with emotional power.*

- *But keep your emotional power from strengthening the doubt and fear in your consciousness.*

- *Clearly dominant, negative emotions can lead to ill health particularly when you know your predominant thoughts are toxic yet you give them permission to thrive in your consciousness.*

__Human Suffering__ - Much human suffering results from the distress of negative emotions that arise from poor social interaction. These include anger, resentment, hatred, lust, aversion and jealousy. As painful as these can be, the extent of pain is actually under the control of the sufferer.

You should know that you have the willpower to restrain negative emotions and to limit their impact upon you. Your emotions are to be your __servants__ not your __masters__.

It may not always be easy to redirect your emotions. It is often best achieved by prayer or distractions such as exercise, watching movies, listening to music, and other ways to get your mind off an emotionally charged situation.

As noted, the four faculties of the soul (Mind, Will, Emotions and Spirit) described above each contain numerous similar capacities.

V. Departure at Death

Our souls will depart our bodies at death and move closer to, or further from, the divine mystery of God, -- depending on our __developed level__ of __faith__ and __spiritual character__ at the time we depart this dimension. Near-death experiences (NDEs) point to the __transcendence__ of our souls.

A Gallup survey recorded that nearly eight million adults in the U.S. have experienced a NDE that included some or all of the following characteristics:[6]

1. *A lifeless physical body showing no heartbeat, no brain waves and no breathing (clinical death)*
2. *Out-of-body experience often involving a tunnel*
3. *Accurate visual and auditory perception while out of body*
4. *Feelings of peace and painlessness*
5. *Visits to another dimension described as heaven*
6. *Encounters with other non-physical beings and a being of light*
7. *Life review*

In his book The Upward Yearnings of the Soul, Dr. Robert Spitzer cites numerous verified, scientific, peer-reviewed studies involving over a thousand patients with NDEs providing "significant verifiable evidence of the survival of human trans-physical consciousness (the soul) after death."[7] NDE studies reveal that the soul of a clinically dead person leaves the body, and initially remains in the vicinity of their body looking down at it.

Those experiencing NDEs say the soul is self-conscious with the ability to see, hear, and retain and recall memories. It is not subject to physical laws like gravity, and it may be pulled, often through a tunnel, to a different spiritual dimension where it might encounter other spiritual beings like itself or a being of intense light. It can communicate with other beings without voice or sound, but does not seem to be in control of its location, eventually being returned (reluctantly) to its body.

Spitzer notes three ways of verifying the experiences of the thousands of patients with documented near-death experiences:

1. Veridical reports - in which activities are observed by the soul of a clinically dead body usually in the operating room or waiting room and 100% verified as having taken place while the soul's body exhibited no signs of life. Such was a case involving the location of a man's false teeth that had been misplaced by a nurse while the man was in a deep coma. The patient's soul had observed where the nurse had placed the dentures, and once the patient was brought back to life, he pointed out the location of his teeth.[8] In another case, a woman accurately described the mismatched attire of her little girl in the waiting room.[9]

*2. Visual perception of the blind - some studies have verified that patients, **blind from birth,** have been able to accurately describe the sight of activity in the operating room and elsewhere while having a near-death experience.[10] Dr. Kenneth Ring and others found in their studies that 80 percent of blind people with near-death experiences had accurate visual perception while physically dead.*

3. Personal information about long deceased individuals - studies have verified personal information about people who died before a patient was born that the patient was able to recall from a near-death experience.

These verified instances of observations and encounters by the souls of patients with no signs of life, (who died on the operating table) dispel the theories of physical causation of near-death experiences due to drugs, hallucinations or wishful thinking of dying brain cells.

This is because purely physical theories cannot explain how dead patients can report verified activity, how the blind can see and how patients can acquire information unknown to them about long dead relatives all during a time when the patients' body is clearly lifeless. The obvious conclusion is that we are souls that can survive the death of our bodies.

Most people realize they exist as a conscious being from their own direct awareness of themselves making conscious choices to direct their bodies to take physical actions. Actions that in fact result in the action chosen such as walking, sitting, eating etc. They are also aware occasionally of themselves thinking about which choices to make in life, - - as in here I am again trying to decide what to have for dinner.[11]

Interestingly, philosopher and theologian J.P. Moreland, says animals have a soul, but it is not as richly structured as the human soul. It does not bear the image of God, and it is far more dependent on the animal's body and sense organs than is the human soul.[12] On the other hand, author and sociologist Ernest Becker points out that man is cursed with a burden no animal has to bear: he is conscious that his own end is inevitable.[13]

The closer I get to the end of my pilgrimage,
the more certain I become of the existence of God.

VI. Summary

You are an eternal soul completely engaged in pervasive, functional integration with your human body. The complexity of both your brain and your soul equate to an interaction of compound complexity.

The soul itself has an extremely complex structure which combines and integrates sensations, thoughts, purposes, desires, and beliefs and makes possible rationality, language, and genuine moral agency.[14]

Personality, character, and intellectual outlook function both consciously and unconsciously.

Mental States of the soul include Sensation, Thought, Belief, Desire and Willful Action. Faculties are the Spirit, the Mind, the Will and the Emotions. Among properties of the soul are Consciousness, Character, Transcendence and Conscience.

Improving our spiritual character is the main reason for our earthly journeys. Spiritual character influences our human attitudes and personality, and its woven into much of what we say and do.

Your mind is the battlefield of your soul, so be very careful what you view, read and listen to, think about and entertain in your mind because corruption, fear and evil will surely try to slip into your consciousness and growing over time it will try to lead you into vice and addiction.

*Your free will is the force of **personal drive** and **self-determination** that allows you to function independently of God and other beings on earth. Free will allows you to choose freely. Choose not spiritual squalor.*

*Each day under the pressure of living human life, we must decide what kind of eternal souls we will become. We do so by making the selfish or unselfish right or wrong choices and behaviors that continue to mold and shape the identity, character and spiritual fiber of our souls. Therefore, it is the **way** we **conduct** our lives that matters most.*

As a temporary member of the human race, you share with all those who have gone before you a great heritage founded on the principles of courage, endurance and a striving to overcome great odds and adversity. You can improve your soul by attaining wisdom, living honorably and improving the quality of life for those around you.

When the Doctor ended his lesson, Warden uncharacteristically stepped forward and said, "I would like to join your cause though I see you have only a small number of helpers with you."

"It is true that I keep few assistants," said the doctor, "but it happens that I have need of one with a cell phone and inexpensive transportation not to mention one that might be skilled in the arts of self-defense."

Warden was thrilled and explained that his old motorcycle got great gas mileage and that he had a good cell phone. After asking Warden about his past and his hopes for the future, he was accepted and encouraged that a place would be found for Carter as well.

The next evening, Carter once more met with Dr. Moses, who was pleased to see him again. The Doctor's face was calm and full of kindness, and he invited Carter to join his small team.

Carter said, "I would like to thank you for even considering me for a position with your organization. However, I feel that I must continue my travels to apply what I have learned thus far on my quest and to put through the living experience what I have learned in theory.

"I really appreciated your teaching on the soul's anatomy because everything you said seemed very clear to me."

"Thank you," said the doctor, "I have spent a lot of time thinking and praying for understanding about it."

"Teachings can be the blueprints for a successful life. However, at some point we have to build the real structure of our lives based upon the blueprint. It is my goal," said Carter, "to build the life as I learn the teachings, so I do not remain always in the classroom when there is so much to put into practice."

With a smile, Dr. Moses looked into Carter's eyes and said, "You are gaining wisdom son. May God be with you on your journey."

"Without a soul, a human being is little more than a few dollars' worth of common chemicals."[15]

Carter knew he would miss Warden a great deal, however from the enlightened physician, he had learned valuable knowledge about the anatomy of his soul. Nevertheless, this valuable knowledge has come at a great cost, for he feared he would never see Warden again.

Be kind to people, for within their souls all are fighting a hard battle.
…Great Greek philosopher Plato

1988 Vatican 200-lira coin depicting Genesis 2:7
"And the Lord God formed man of the dust of the ground and breathed into his nostril the breath of life; and man became a living soul"

God may want a community of souls of sufficiently holy and righteous character to be able to exist undamaged in the infinitely powerful force-field of his ultra-pure, holy and sacred presence. In the extreme, radiating, spiritual energy of Divinity, souls of contaminated character with spiritually combustible material (sin) may be burned to ashes or explode like popcorn in a microwave oven. Therefore, **we live this life to develop a soul of more honorable character worthy of a safer and closer relationship to God.**

The impact of being in God's presence will depend on what your soul is made of, somewhat like the effects of the sun hardenings and preserving a pot of clay, but melting and destroying a candle of wax.

Souls Trapped in Bodies

According to the proverbs of Solomon, the wisest of kings,
God preserves those who have the desire for wisdom, understanding and
truth, and who want very much to lead an honest life of righteous virtue
despite the innumerable temptations to do otherwise.
...Proverbs 2:1-22

---

[1] From the gospel song "I'll Fly Away" attributed to Albert Edward Brumley

[2] S. Goetz & C. Taliaferro, *A Brief History of the Soul*, Wiley Blackwell, Oxford, p.158

[3] Caroline Myss, *Anatomy of the Spirit*, Crown Publishers 1996, p.67

[4] C.S. Lewis, *The Great Divorce*, Macmillan Company, 1952.

[5] James Allen, *As a Man Thinketh*, DeVorass & Co., Marina Del Rey, CA 1950

[6] George Gallup Jr. and William Proctor, *Adventures in Immortality*, New York, McGraw-Hill, 1982

[7] Robert Spitzer, *The Soul's Upward Yearning*, San Francisco, Ignatius Press, 2015, Chapter 5

[8] Ibid p. 191

[9] Raymond A. Moody, *Light Beyond*, New York, Bantam Books, 1998, pp.17-20

[10] Robert Spitzer, *The Soul's Upward Yearning*, San Francisco, Ignatius, 2015, p. 193

[11] S. Goetz & C. Taliaferro, *A Brief History of the Soul*, Wiley Blackwell, Oxford, p.176

[12] Moreland, J.P., *The Soul: How We Know It's Real:* Chicago: Moody, 2014, p.120

[13] Becker, Ernest, *Escape from Evil*, New York, Free Press, 1975, p.3

[14] John W. Cooper, *Body, Soul, and Life Everlasting*, Kindle Edition, 2705

[15] An estimate of the value of the chemicals making up the human body is about $160 per http://www.datagenetics.com/blog/ April 2011.

Keep your soul in exercise,
lest her faculties rust for want of motion;
to dwell too long in the employments of the body
is both the cause and the sign of a dull spirit.
...Wellins Calcott, Thoughts Moral and Divine

Chapter 3
<u>The Soul of Joy and Happiness</u>

Carter leaves the Athens Park, Warden and the good Doctor Moses in search of more spiritual enlightenment about the human soul. At times, he has an uncanny feeling that he is being followed. However, after circling back a couple of times and finding no one, he mistakenly assumes he is just missing Warden.

Despite the doctor's excellent description of the anatomy of the soul, Carter feels he needs a better understanding of other aspects of his soul, so he reviews what he has learned thus far.

- From his grandfather, the Colonel, he learned that he is a unique and potentially awesome life form capable of learning to use spiritual power.

- He realized that his mind is a battleground where the spiritual forces of honor and virtue are constantly engaged against forces of temptation and corruption.

- He understands that the **thoughts** he entertains in his mind will **determine** if he is strong or weak, happy or unhappy, good or bad, wise or foolish. In addition, he has learned to control his thoughts with spiritual force and willpower.

- He recognized that he is a **three-part being** consisting of a physical body inhabited by a soul with a spiritual life force.

- He realized that his duty is to emerge from this life with a soul of **more mature, positive and holy character** than the possibly untested one with which he entered this world.

- He believes human life is an opportunity for his soul **to learn** to live more in faith, with hope and courage and without negativity, selfishness and fear.

Carter understands that his mission and purpose in life should include:

1. Citizenship as **duties to** the **society** in which he lives

2. Determining and fulfilling his earthly **destiny** or **destinies**

3. Becoming the very best he can be in **his roles** in this life

4. Developing the spiritual maturity for a closer personal **relationship with the Divine Order, to accept fully God's grace** and to be **at peace with Him**

About his soul's anatomy, Carter has learned that his soul consists of four parts and associated properties:

1. His **Spirit** - the eternal life force that energizes his physical body in the earthly realm and is the conscious force that is life itself

2. His immortal **Mind** - his thinking and memory component

3. His **Will** - his will power, personal drive and **self-determination**

4. His **Emotions** - the passions of his soul, establishing the feelings in his consciousness that collectively create his changing moods

5. Among the properties of his soul are its Consciousness, Transcendence, Character and Conscience.

Finally, he had come to realize that his spiritual **character** is an **eternal work in progress,** that helps shape his daily moral and ethical choices and is itself **shaped by** those same choices.

Still Carter is not satisfied that he really understands the full nature of his soul, his very essence, that part of him that will live through eternity.

> "Money will not buy happiness,
> but it will let you be unhappy in nicer places."
> *...Unknown*

Carter has always been a serious young man and his years with the ascetics have only amplified that tendency. Nevertheless, he wonders about the evident joy and happiness that he so often observes in most other young people.

There seems to be a carefree attitude among many people of his generation. They appear to live happily for the moment from one laugh to the next.

In fact, Carter begins to wonder if perhaps joy and happiness might be important windows into his soul that he has thus far completely overlooked. After all, he recalls that one ancient sage, Aristotle, thought happiness was the purpose of life. He also recalls that joy should be an important property of the human spirit.

Carter calls and discusses his thoughts about happiness with his grandfather, who agrees that it could very well provide significant insight into the soul of humankind. "Happiness has been likened to the once natural, hale and hardy state of the human soul," says the Colonel. "Perhaps," he adds, "we should find out more about what it takes to make human beings happy."

They decide to review all the research they can find on human happiness, so Carter returns home and moves in with his grandparents to begin their investigation into the nature and causes of joy and happiness in people.

One night not long after Carter returns home, his grandfather's new car is vandalized with deflated tires, scratched paint and broken windows. Carter has been driving it since returning home, mostly just to the library or to church. They assume it is the work of neighborhood kids and turn it over to the insurance company after reporting it to the police. However, Carter has a nagging feeling there's more to it.

The next evening about 9:30, Carter and his grandfather are talking seated in a small front room of the Colonel's house. Suddenly, the front window explodes, sending glass flying across the room like buckshot, as a brick flies through the window and lands with a thud on the floor against the far wall.

Carter dashes to the door as the Colonel douses the lights, but there is nothing to see but a dark vehicle speeding out of sight. Taped to the brick is a typed note that says, "We know where you are, and we do not forget."

Carter tells the Colonel that he suspects the vandalized car and the brick are the work of a domestic terrorist group known as APOLLYON. Thinking back, he figures he was followed home from the park in Athens by a member of the APOLLYON network.

Carter explained that the APOLLYON movement is a network of left wing autonomous, militant anti-God groups that try to advance their socialist political agenda through violence and intimidation. He further explains that they were after Dr. Moses who Carter and Warden helped defend.

"I presume that is what they mean by we do not forget," says Carter.

The Colonel says he is ready for a good fight if the cowards will come out in the open. Still feisty in his seventies, he loads his double-barreled shotgun, activates his alarm systems and lets his black and tan German Shepherd named Chase out of the house to prowl the grounds.

"You know," adds the bespectacled former economics professor, "it's a shame more people don't understand enough economics to realize what an extremely powerful force capitalism can be. It creates greater prosperity for all through the potent incentives of freedom and self-interest that motivate a nation's people to work hard to become the best they can be. Thereby producing more opportunity and success for everyone – the way a rising tide lifts all boats."

"On the other hand, Socialism and Communism stamp out and destroy the critical personal incentives of freedom and self-interest. They are replaced instead with government control and government's interest. With that government control, comes human rights abuse."

The Colonel continues, "Taking too much from those who produce and giving it to those who do not produce only destroys everyone's incentive to be productive. That in turn, reduces prosperity for all. History is littered with the corpses of nations that have tried socialism and communism only to end up with wrecked economies, much poorer people and a few wealthy, corrupt dictators like Hitler, Stalin, Mao or Castro at the top.

"I guess APOLLYON like the Socialist and Communist before them promise spreading the wealth for all, which sounds good except that the missing incentives eventually reduce and eliminate the wealth until there is nothing to spread but poverty. By then of course, APOLLYON will be the corrupt ones at the top living on the backs of everyone else.

"Ah well, let's pray they don't get away with it," he adds.

After weeks of extensive research, Carter and the Colonel conclude that happiness is indeed an important attribute of a healthy soul. They complete the next three chapters about human happiness for the Handbook of the Soul.

"When someone gets something for nothing; someone else gets nothing for something."
...*Bits & Pieces*

<u>Handbook of the Soul</u>

Secrets of a
Joyful and Happy Soul

I. Preview

- *Human happiness is affected by countless factors.*

- *Happiness in life is measured as both the joy of the moment or satisfaction with life over time.*

- *Happiness, partly genetic, is considered to be from 40% to 60% within **our control**.[1]*

- *Successful relationships among people contribute greatly to human happiness.*

- *Finding **increased meaning** in what we do and increasing our level of **engagement** are major avenues to greater happiness.*

II. Introduction

Although some governments guarantee their citizens the right to life, liberty and the pursuit of happiness, they do not define happiness or explain how to get it. In addition, government cannot guarantee happiness, only the right to pursue it. In this chapter, we will try to define human happiness and determine some of what makes us happy.

The joy in our souls both affects and is affected by our level of happiness and our general satisfaction with our lives. As the following research indicates, much of our happiness lies within our control.

Our contentment, our success in the workplace and our impact on our friends and family are significantly affected by our personal level of happiness.

According to the research team at Trends Inc., happiness in human life is important for the following reasons: [2]

"Happiness does not depend on outward things, but on the way we see them"
...Author Leo Tolstoy

- *"At the societal level, happy populations engage in less crime, terrorism or political revolts."*

- *"At the organizational level, research consistently shows happy employees to be more productive, even though happiness is just one of many factors involved."*

- *"At the individual level, a person's happiness plays an enormous role in determining how successful he or she will be in their relations with other people including family. It also determines how satisfying the experience of success will feel to the individual."*

Throughout human history, the desire for happiness has been great, but happiness is known to be a subjective, intangible and sometimes elusive condition.

The human experience on earth is not designed to be an endless festival of joy and happiness, because we are here to develop virtuous spiritual character, and that must come about through adversity as well as success.

Nevertheless, an important trait of mature spiritual character is the ability to remain relatively happy, joyful and positive in spite of life's challenges and difficulties. Doing so is a noble endeavor, and after all, it's much more fun being happy than unhappy.

*Research has shown that, although our individual inherited personality traits determine part of our ability to enjoy happiness, human beings can also exercise a great deal of **control over** their **own levels** of happiness.*

It is very important to realize that the external circumstances and other people in our lives have much less to do with our happiness than the manner in which we respond to them.

- *It is also essential to recognize that the human response to most situations is largely a **matter of choice**.*

"Every soul is a battlefield."
...Author Lyman Abbott in "Problems of Life"

- *Your response to a situation can be positive or negative.*

- *If you apply sufficient will power, your response to most of life's ups and downs can be positive. A habit of reacting positively to life's challenges and opportunities inevitably leads to more happiness in life.*

You can condition your soul to be the positive, creative leader of your being by adopting a positive attitude and shunning negative talk and negative people. Alternatively, a habit of reacting negatively to life's challenges and opportunities makes for a negative person who is likely to find very little happiness in life or work.

- *Life is about choices, and spiritual character is built with the choices humans make.*

- *It is, therefore, worth the effort to develop a habit of responding to most situations in a positive way by making positive choices.*

If you are basically unhappy in one set of circumstances, you may be unhappy in different circumstances as well.

- *This is because your overall settled sense of happiness results more from the **character of your soul** and your genetic inheritance than from the external circumstances of life.*

- *The good news is that both circumstance and character can be improved. Although, in the end, it is only the improvement in character that matters.*

III. Definition and Measurement

Happiness research has defined and measured human happiness in a couple of ways: [3]

"The greater part of our happiness or misery depends on our dispositions and not on our circumstances."
...Martha Washington[4]

1. *Happiness has been measured as the **level of joy** that exists **in** your **daily moods** sampled and averaged over time.*

- *This provides an indication of the quantity of joy actually experienced on a day-to-day basis as a percentage of your total feelings.*

- *Joy is a very positive, upbeat human emotional state, and a very powerful spiritual force that you must develop, confess and live by if you want to enjoy its power.*

2. *Human happiness has also been defined and measured as the **overall level of satisfaction** you have with your life.*

- *This is more a reflection about the qualitative level of **satisfaction** or **settled happiness** with **life in general** as remembered **across time**.*

- *We tend to remember the high and low points and the way things end when we reflect back on experiences.*

- *Therefore, your level of remembered happiness or overall satisfaction with life can be quite different from the average level of joy you actually experience in your various moods each day.*

IV. Happiness doesn't just happen to us

- *Happiness is a **mindset** that we have a moral duty to establish as part of the formation and configuration of our souls. Our happiness affects other people because happy people treat one another better, have better marriages and are better citizens.[5]*

- *We must actively train ourselves to **seek satisfaction** from work, from what we can contribute to society and from fellowship with family, friends and other people.*

**Happy relationships depend not on finding the right person,
but on being the right person.**
...Eric Butterworth.

V. Characteristics of Human Happiness

1. *Happiness is **not a constant state**. It is obvious that happiness in individuals **varies up** and **down** and is related to several factors including your age.* [6]

2. *As much as half of your satisfaction in life could be influenced by your inherited traits such as personality, ability to handle stress and inherited tendencies toward joy, anxiety or depression.*

   - *However, studies on identical and fraternal twins found that even when people have the same genetic makeup, some are much happier than others.*

   - *Thus, much of human happiness appears to be well within the individual's control.* [7]

3. *The half or more of the factors driving your happiness are well **within your control** and can be attributed to the ways in which you deal with your challenges and opportunities. Experts are seeing happiness more as a talent than an inborn trait.* [8]

   - *Some of these factors related to levels of human happiness include the quality of human relationships, religious faith and job satisfaction.*

   - *Also important is the amount of negativity feeding your mind, your willingness to bounce back from temporary setbacks, and to some extent your level of income, marital status and education.*

4. *Your happiness may **vary with your age**. Adult women tend to become less happy up to their mid-40s after which they tend to become happier as they get older. With men it's in their early 50s.*

   - *As we age, we often experience disappointments with our lives not meeting all our dreams. By our mid-40s to 50s we may have more realistic expectations.*

   - *Children are usually older and people have a little more time for themselves by their forties and fifties.*

- *Multitasking tends to be mentally stressful, detracting from our sense of wellbeing over time. Keeping our minds on what we are doing and trying to enjoy it (mindfulness) helps.*

5. *In spite of changed circumstances, happiness levels for most human beings tend to **return to** normal fairly soon after reacting to positive or negative situations depending on our level of resiliency.*

   - *Exceptions are the loss of a spouse or the loss of a job. After which, it may take years for your happiness to return to its original level.*

   - *Resilience can become a learned skill if you train your brain to regulate its response to stress and fear.*

6. *In the human experience, good fortune or good luck sometimes runs in cycles, with several days or weeks in which everything goes well in life. Often followed by similar periods when many things tend to go wrong.*

   The most important thing to remember about down cycles, about being in a rut or suffering the pain of great loss is that, given time, these things will pass, and life will feel good again.

   - *The passage of **time heals all things**, and it is critical to keep that perspective when in the depths of emotional pain and despair.*

   - *Depression can set in when the human spirit loses hope.*

   - *However, hope should never die in those who remember that time heals all things and "this too shall pass."*

   - *When things are not going well, the sooner you can apply faith that things will get better, the sooner things will look up again.*

7. *We need to realize that we must accept **responsibility for our own lives** because we can control much of what happens to us: by the way we think, choose and act.*

   - *Even when we are challenged by what we cannot control, the way we choose to bear our burdens is within our control.*

- *We have an obligation as human beings of dignity and choice to make the best of every situation because with hope and positive energy, we can often turn challenges into triumphs.*

8. *In many respects, happiness is **relative to expectations and reality.***

   - *People who are accustomed to having nothing can be happy with very little.*

   - *People accustomed to having everything they want may find it difficult to be happy with just a little less.*

   - *Happiness can also be affected by the difference between your expectations and reality. Expect the best but not the impossible.*

9. *Joy and pleasure tend to be of a **transient nature,** because, although they result from many human activities, they do not necessarily continue with a steady continuation of the same activities.*

   - *Over time, the pleasure often diminishes in intensity until the activity becomes boring, providing little joy or happiness.*

   - *On the other hand, pleasurable activities can be cycled over time in such a way that they continue to produce pleasure each time the activity is renewed.*

10. *Happy and unhappy moods are **contagious** and can affect the moods of other people.*

11. *The human spirit has a way of adjusting over time to most any constant circumstance or continuing condition, and it can become bored even with a constant state of happiness. To appreciate happiness fully, you **must also experience unhappiness.***

12. *Good human character dictates an **unselfish responsibility** to make all things, at all times, as cheerful and comfortable **for others** as possible. Doing things to help other people is a sure cure for your own unhappiness.*

- *Human beings have a mutual moral duty to avoid negativity, strife and emotional discord. You should resist the ignoble and selfish pull of your own negative moods and take special care **not to bring others down**.*

- *It is important to use emotional discipline to avoid being grouchy, depressed, upset, irritated or angry, especially in the company of others.*

13. *In the human brain, an increase of neural activity in the left prefrontal cortex has been associated with the state of happiness.[9]*

14. *Your happiness level can be raised permanently through conscious effort. Some steps to greater happiness are described in the following section.*

VI. Steps to Greater Happiness

1. ***Develop A More Positive Attitude***: *Your outlook on life can be improved by striving to develop and maintain a more positive attitude.*

    - *It has been said that, attitude has more impact on life than the past, than facts, than education, than money, than circumstances, than failures, than successes, than what other people think, say or do.*

    - *Attitude is more important than appearance, giftedness or skill.*

    - *Attitude will make or break a home or a company.*

    The remarkable thing is that we have a choice every day regarding the attitude we will embrace for that day.

    - *"We cannot change our past, and we cannot change the fact that other people will act in a certain way.*

    - *"We cannot change the inevitable.*

    - *"The only thing we can do is depend on the one asset we have, and that is our attitude.*

- *"I am convinced that life is 10% what happens to us and 90% how we react to it."[10]*

Negativity Trap *- It is essential that we do whatever it takes to **avoid** becoming an overly critical person with a negative outlook that will lead us down a path of growing negativity into a self-reinforcing negativity trap.*

However, if we find ourselves already trapped in negativity it is important to know how to escape. There are ways of improving one's attitude even for faultfinding pessimists.

- *It requires dogged persistence to keep at it until, over time, more positive thoughts lead to more positive words and actions.*

- *With repetition, the more positive words and actions become internalized as positive habits, leading eventually to a more positive attitude.*

As we go through life, we are learning, adapting and constantly evolving into new people.

- *Our souls and brains must be able to maintain a sense of self-identity while facilitating all the growth and change of a human life without losing sight of who we are.*

- *The brain does so by constantly rewiring the connections between neurons and possibly even changing their functions in a process known as neuroplasticity.*

Neuroscientist Dr. Andrew Newberg M.D. in his book The Spiritual Brain: Science and Religious Experience, points out that over time positive thinking and practices rewire the brain in ways that dispose it to more positive thinking.

- *Likewise, sustained negative thinking rewires and organizes our brains for more negative thinking.*

- *Using neuroplasticity, the brain constantly reorganizes its neural networks to better facilitate the kind of thinking it finds itself doing most often.*

Newberg notes, "Negative thoughts activate the brain structures associated with negative emotions and create a stress response.

- *"The more the brain thinks negative thoughts, the stronger negative neural connections become.*

- *"In other words, negativity leads to more negativity, and that in turn affects the brain's organization."* [11]

In the same way, positive thoughts and emotions activate areas of the brain that are involved with happiness and reward, lowering the stress response and improving memory and behavior.

- *Thus, positive thinking leads to more positive thinking, as the brain rewires itself to facilitate and accommodate more positive thought.*

- *Therefore, the way out of the negativity trap is to use neuroplasticity to reorganize our thinking.*

- *We do so by focusing on the positive and shunning the negative for 30 to 90 days or until we can tell that our minds have become more interested in the positive instead of the negative.* [12]

- *We must then be vigilant that we not fall back into negativity, for there is constant temptation to do so.*

It is obvious that people with a positive attitude, who are predisposed to look on the sunny side of life, are definitely happier than people with a less positive outlook. The greatest detractors from human happiness tend to be attitudes of selfishness, fear, negativity or ingratitude.

They can sneak up and gradually take over the interior dynamics of your attitude until you see everything through lenses of selfishness, fear or negativity.

- *You can become a "carrier" of these "illnesses of attitude" spreading them to other susceptible people who may be among your family, friends and coworkers.*

- *A negative attitude deepens disappointments, undermines pleasure, happiness and satisfaction, and it may lead to depression or physical illness.*

- *A positive attitude on the other hand enables people to endure suffering and disappointment and enhances their enjoyment and satisfaction in life.*

More on a positive attitude will be found in book 5 of this series.

Founding father Ben Franklin said, Happiness consists more in small conveniences or pleasures that occur every day, than in great pieces of good fortune that happen but seldom to a person in the course of his or her life.

2. <u>Increase Meaning</u>: *Settled happiness or satisfaction with life will be much greater for you if you find meaning and purpose in your life.*

- *The way we handle everything from big challenges to everyday situations helps shape the meaning of our lives.*

- *Humans are **self-determining** beings.*

- *We create what we become within the broad limits of our genetic endowment and our environment.*

- *We do so by the thoughts we think, the choices we make and the actions we take.*

To attain more meaning in life, we must get beyond the mere attainment of personal pleasures.

We must focus on doing more things that are directed toward something or someone other than ourselves by giving ourselves a cause to serve or a person to love.[13]

> **"A merry heart does good like a medicine:**
> **but a broken spirit dries the bones."**
> *...Proverbs 17:22*

- *You can find more meaning in life by dedicating part of your time and talent to **meaningful causes** that are centered on helping others less fortunate than yourself.*

- *A cause should be something you can **get involved in** and care about deeply, something that eventually grabs your soul and inspires your behavior.*

This could be accomplished by joining a church, helping the local animal shelter, helping the Salvation Army, joining any of the many service organizations like the Lions, Civitan or Rotary, running for local political office or joining the campaigns of those who do.

Other options are becoming a foster parent, volunteering for mentoring, or for helping in the local schools, volunteering to help at the local library, or hospital. In addition, becoming a volunteer firefighter, joining the police auxiliary or finding a way to join a group supporting any cause worth believing in.

*In her book The Choice Is Yours, Helen Macinness points out that **nothing is interesting if you're not interested.**[14] Therefore, you may need to make the effort to become interested in something.*

Many people start part time businesses to meet needs they feel passionate about by providing a product or service for which people would gladly pay.

3. Increase Engagement: *It has been said that life should be lived with so much zest that at death one should be like an exhausted ballplayer sliding sideways into home plate yelling Yahoo! What a great trip!*

- *Although, not every moment of life should be filled with excitement, you should be very interested, fully engaged and deeply caring about some of the things you do with your life.*

- *The difference between meaning and engagement is that **meaning** is associated with **purpose in life,** while **engagement** means the **extent of involvement or participation** in whatever you are doing.*

- *It would be most fulfilling to be **heavily engaged** in activities that are **meaningful** to you.*

*Engagement can be increased by becoming more **deeply involved** in whatever you are doing by serving on committees at work, for example, or by serving as the treasurer, secretary or president in the other kinds of organizations and clubs to which you may belong.*

- *Half the time we are not actually thinking about what we are doing, meaning we are not fully engaged in it. Engagement can mean taking on more responsibility in whatever you are doing.*

- *You can increase your level of **commitment and involvement** with work, family or friends.*

Engagement with life can be increased also by joining clubs, taking up hobbies, taking courses of interest, starting a part time business, traveling, camping, learning sports like skiing, martial arts, tennis, golf, etc.

4. **Increase Gratitude**: *Counting your blessings can have a significant impact on your level of happiness.*

- *Gratitude can be greatly enhanced by using a diary or gratitude journal to write down things to be appreciative and thankful for each week.*

- *In addition, gratitude can be enhanced by remembering a few things each day to be thankful for in prayer.*

5. **Connect with Other People:** *One of the fundamental finding from the science of happiness is that almost every human being feels happier when they're with other people.*

- *It seems paradoxical because in our fast-paced lives, many people can hardly wait to get home and be alone with nothing to do.*

"There is no duty we so much underrate as the duty of being happy. By being happy, we sow anonymous benefits upon the world."
... Author Robert Louis Stevenson

- *However, if alone for very long with nothing to do, the quality of most people's experience really plummets.*[15]

Harvard University professor Robert Putnam says 50 years of research shows that people with the best relationships with other people are the happiest.

- *People with good relationships with the other people in their lives are more likely to live longer and healthier lives.*

- *"The highest levels of happiness are found with the most stable, longest and most contented relationships."*[16]

- *Most people said purchasing experiences are a better value for happiness than purchasing things.*

- *When asked to look back on past purchases, 83% of people said their biggest regret was passing up an experience they could have had such as a trip with friends.*[17]

- *This is probably because mutual experiences are more likely to make us feel more connected to others.*

"Buying a giant flat screen TV may make us happy as we walk out of the store, but what we are buying is an implicit commitment to plunking ourselves in front of it – often alone – for one-sixth of the next year.

- *"In every study, people who watch more television are less satisfied with their lives than people who watch less TV."*[18]

- *It seems clear that good social relationships are emerging as the foundation of happiness.*

6. ***Improve Interpersonal Skills:*** *Efforts to develop strong interpersonal communications skills, such as sensitivity and empathy toward others can pay off.*

"Humor is to life what shock absorbers are to automobiles."
...Comic Dennis Waitley

- *Improved interpersonal virtues like kindness, gratitude and capacity for love can result in greater happiness by increasing the enjoyment and satisfaction of being with other people.*

- *Again, decades of research indicate that people who have the best relationships with other people are much happier than those who do not.[19]*

7. **Learn to Forgive**: *To harbor **resentment** is to harbor **unhappiness**, but to forgive freely is to enjoy freedom and happiness.*

   - *Your reaction to the actions of other people affects your own character, which is shaped by the many small choices you make each day.*

   - *Forgiveness benefits the **forgiver** more than the forgiven.*

8. **Reduce Avoidable Stress:** *Think about the pressures in life that are creating stress and reduce as many as possible.*

   Get better organized, spend less time watching the news or other stress inducing television shows, and be aware of the stressful and habit-forming nature of most electronic games.

   - *Cut back on activities and commitments enough to schedule "down time" each day for doing things that provide personal relaxation such as walking, reading, listening to soothing music, stretching or breathing exercises, soaking in the tub or whatever else provides complete relaxation.*

   - *Those in high stress jobs should be extra careful to take their vacation days and holidays since one purpose of days off is to provide a break, and most people are not only happier, but also more productive after getting a break from their work.*

   - *All humans experience stress, and reasonable levels of stress are part of life.*

"Happiness when shared is never reduced"
... Siddhārtha Gautama

- *It should not, however, take a constant diet of caffeine or drugs to cope with the daily schedule.*

- *When stress creates constant anxiety, depression or a sense of being driven without pause by the demands of a life that feels out of control, then stress is likely to be at harmful levels.*

It is much better to get stress under control early than to deal with the mental and emotional breakdowns or damage to the body's nervous system that can result from a lifestyle of excess stress.

*Some common **symptoms** of excess stress include the following:*

- *Irritability*

- *Strained relationships*

- *Overreacting to little things*

- *Fatigue*

- *Constipation*

- *Insomnia*

- *Headaches*

- *Tension aches between the shoulders at the base of the neck*

- *Lower backaches*

There are several basic human personality types (determined by personality tests) that react differently to stress:

- *Type A, which tends to be the more intense, highly motivated, overachiever type*

- *The type B personality, on the other hand, is more laid back, relaxed and easier going.*

- *Many human personalities are a combination.*

- *Some personality types enable human beings to deal better with stress than others.*

- *It can be helpful to understand your personality type because what reduces stress for some personality types does not do so for others.*

Top stress reducers that work for most people include:

- *Deep breathing and relaxation techniques*
- *Adequate sleep*
- *A healthy diet including fish*
- *Exercise*
- *Good posture*
- *Saying "no thanks" to some of the things you are asked to do*
- *A determination to maintain a positive attitude*
- *Caring for other people*
- *Petting your pets & going outside more often*
- *Frequently and affectionately hugging your loved ones*
- *Smiling more often*

Research shows that even a slight loss of sleep can affect memory, judgement and mood causing additional stress.[20]

*Laughter is also a universal **stress buster** because the act of laughing releases endorphins – hormones that trigger feelings of happiness and well-being.*

You don't have to wait until you are happy to laugh and smile, because you can laugh and smile to help make yourself happy.[21]

In addition, human touching reduces stress. Research has shown that married couples that touch each other affectionately for at least 30 minutes three times a week experience 34% lower levels of stress.[22]

9.   *Understand the Limitations of Money:*

In material societies, the stress, strain and hardship of living in poverty can cause human unhappiness. This is more so, if many others in the same society have succeeded in attaining a visibly higher standard of living.

These circumstances can combine the difficulty of scraping to get by with resentment, jealousy and possibly a sense of personal failure.

A paper published in the Journal of Personality and Social Psychology, compared the happiness levels of people who had been paralyzed in an accident with people who had won the lottery compared to a control group who had neither been paralyzed nor won a lottery.

- *Those that were paralyzed were somewhat less happy than were those in the control group.[23]*

- *Lottery winners, however, were no happier than the control group.*

Research indicates that happiness can be affected by the amount of money one earns up to a point.

Once your basic needs are met and a middle-class level of income is achieved, more money might have less effect on your basic sense of satisfaction with life.

The rising affluence of developed countries has led to widespread material prosperity accompanied by the secularization of human society with little increase in personal satisfaction or settled levels of happiness.[24]

- *People are considerably less happy in very poor countries.*

- *Among the more prosperous and happier countries, however, the level of happiness has not kept pace as the level of real income has grown beyond a reasonably prosperous level.*

Research by Trends Inc. finds that rising income will only have a positive effect on happiness if aspirations or desires do not rise even more quickly.

- *If people make more money, they can be happier.*

- *However, if they are constantly disappointed because they expected to make even more money, then rising income might not help.*

- *Therefore, happiness is also a matter of managing your financial expectations, so that aspirations remain realistic and attainable.[25]*

No matter how wealthy people become, they tend over time to **adjust to their new circumstances.** After a while, they begin to compare what they have to other wealthy people in their new peer group and may eventually lose the happiness of their newfound wealth.

- *However, regardless of their level of income, most people believe they need a little more than they have to live well.*

- *On the other hand, people of all income levels tend to be happier and more satisfied, as long as they think the prospects for their lot in life are improving.*

Additional income **does** seem to bring more happiness if it is used to **invest in** things that of themselves increase happiness.

- *Such things as giving to favorite charities, spending more time with loved ones or improvements in your health seem to increase happiness.*

- *Studies reportedly show that 5% of people in poor health say they are happy, where as 50% of those in excellent health say they are happy.[26]*

Beyond earning, enough to stay out of poverty, stay healthy and retire comfortably, money, with a few exceptions, can't buy real happiness because in the human experience the things that bring the **most happiness cannot be purchased.**

Author Greg Easterbrook says, "Love, friendship, family, respect, a place in the community, the belief that your life has purpose and faith: these are the essentials of human fulfillment and they cannot be purchased with cash."

Gretchen Rubin, author of the bestselling book The Happiness Project discovered that people can build happiness into their lives through, among other things, good habits, a positive outlook, and very importantly **willed contentment**, which is a function of the soul's will power.[27]

VII. Summary

- *Human happiness is affected by countless factors.*

- *Happiness in life is measured as both the joy of the moment or satisfaction with life over time.*

- *Happiness, partly genetic, is considered to be from 40% to 60% well within **our control**.[28](willed contentment)*

- *Positive attitudes and successful relationships among people contribute greatly to human happiness.*

- *Finding **increased meaning** in what we do and increasing our level of **engagement** are major avenues to greater happiness.*

Several times the Colonel asks Carter about Warden and each time Carter assures him that Warden is in good company. Carter and his grandfather unearth a great deal of research on human happiness the rest of which is summarized in the next two chapters.

"Give More, Expect Less, Live Simply"
...Theologian Robert Schuler

---

[1] Hilke Brockmann, Jan Delhey, *Human Happiness and the Pursuit of Maximization: Is More Always Better?* (Google eBook) 2013 p.119

[2] Trends Magazine- Published on Jan 15, 2014 issue 129

[3] Research by Edward Diener, University of Illinois; Daniel Kahneman, Princeton University; Martin Seligman, University of Pennsylvania; Psychologist Mihaly Csikszen tmihalyi; Sonja Lyubomirskl, University of California.

[4] John Blankenship in the Register-Herald newspaper, Beckley WV, July 14,2006

[5] Arthur C. Brooks, *Gross National Happiness*, Basic Books Perseus Books Group. NY, 2008 p.17.

[6] David Lykken, University of Minnesota

[7] Trends Magazine- Published on Jan 15, 2014 issue 129

[8] Time Magazine, *The Science of Happiness Update 2019, Meredith Corp. NY p.56*

[9] Richard Davidson, University of Wisconsin

[10] Charles Swindoll's Analysis of Attitude referenced in Bob Welch's book *52 Lessons from A Christmas Carol*, Thomas Nelson, Nashville, 2015, p74

[11] Dr. Andrew Newberg, The Spiritual Brain: Science and Religious Experience, ©The Teaching Company 2012 p.146-148

[12] http://www.huffingtonpost.com/james-clear/forming-new-habits_b_5104807.html January 14th 2015

[13] Vicktor Frankel, *Man's Search for Meaning*, Beacon Press; -p.159

[14] Helen Macinness, *The Choice Is Yours*, p57

[15] Psychologist Mihaly Csikszentmihalyi

[16] Sharon Begley for Newsweek reporting on University of Illinois 30-year research in Reader's Digest Oct. 2012.

[17] What Price Experience by Frank Bures in The Rotarian magazine March 2014

[18] Ibid, citing research by Elizabeth Dunn & Michael Norton in their book -*Happy Money: The science of Smarter Spending*

[19] *Trends Magazine, June 2006, Marketing p.1of 4*

[20] Gina Shaw in WebMD magazine Sept. 2015 p63

[21] Bottom Line Personal newsletter, April 1st, 2009, Vol. 30 number 7, p10. Interview with Scott Hamilton

[22] Ibid p15, Research per Julianne Holt-Lunstad, PhD.

[23] *Journal of Personality and Social Psychology,* August 1978, "Lottery Winners and Accident Victims: Is Happiness Relative?" by Philip Brickman, Dan Coates, and Ronnie Janoff-Bulman. © Copyright 1978 by the American Psychological Association. http://education.ucsb.edu

[24] David Meyers, *GOD for the 21st Century*, p101, ISBN I-890151-39-4 edited by Russell Stannard

[25] Trends Magazine- Published on Jan 15, 2014 issue 129

[26] Bottom Line Personal newsletter, September 1st, 2007, p8. columnist M.P. Dunleavey sites University of Pittsburgh study.

[27] David Jeremiah, A Life Beyond Amazing, Thomas Nelson, Nashville,2017, p 24

[28] Hilke Brockmann, Jan Delhey *Human Happiness and the Pursuit of Maximization: Is More Always Better?* P.119 (Google eBook) 2013

"Believe in your possibilities not your limitations!"
...Antony Robbins

Sometimes your joy is the source of your smile. Sometimes, your smile is the source of your joy.
...Thich Nhat Hanh

Chapter 4
Human Happiness
and Satisfaction with Life

C arter and his grandfather have found a wealth of material about happiness that they continue to summarize for the family journal. Carter hopes to find out if carefree happiness can help him gain more insight into his soul.

Carter enjoys the time spent with his mom, dad and grandparents, and he begins to realize the value of a close and caring family. More of their research on happiness follows:

I. Review of Joy and Happiness (from previous chapter)

- *Happiness in life is measured as joy of the moment or satisfaction with life over time.*

- *Your degree of happiness in life is partly inherited; however, 40% to 60% is well within **your control**.*

- *There are great benefits to learning how to be happier with your life and with yourself.*

- *Successful relationships among people contribute greatly to human happiness.*

- *Finding **increased meaning** in what you do and increasing your level of **engagement** are major contributors to greater happiness.*

> **"Evil is the corruption of an otherwise good thing."**
> *...Professor C.S. Lewis*

II. Preview (current chapter)

- *Joy and happiness can result from a great many different human activities.*

- *The specifics of what makes people happy can differ among individuals.*

- *The following factors and activities contribute to happiness in most people.*

III. Happiness Factors

1. ***Happy Young People Become More Prosperous Adults***. *While more money (up to a point) can make us happier, it seems the reverse is also true.*

A study reported in the Proceedings of the National Academy of Sciences analyzed data from 15,000 U.S. adolescents and young adults.

- *The study concluded that young people who describe themselves as happier or more satisfied with their lives are more likely to go on to earn significantly higher levels of income during their careers[1]*

- *According to the research, the greater wealth is largely due to the greater tendency of happy people to earn a college degree, find a satisfying job, and win promotions than people who are less happy.*

- *The study demonstrated that, even among children from the same households and controlling for other factors, such as IQ, education and health, happier siblings earn higher incomes.*

"When one door of happiness closes, another opens,
but often we look so long at the closed door that we do not see
the one which has been opened for us."
… Deaf-blind Author Helen Keller

2. ***Positive Experiences*** - *Ed Diener at the University of Illinois says that **life is judged happy** if we have more positive experiences (an enjoyable job, loving spouse, a hobby, etc.) than negative ones on a day-to-day basis.*

- *In addition, we can **occasionally** manage to have an intensely positive event, such as a new child, a fantastic vacation, public recognition for an achievement, etc.*

- *The **frequency of positive experiences** is **more important**, Diener says, than the intensity of occasional positive events.*

3. ***Consider Pets*** - *Pets, especially those you can interact with like cats and dogs, can dispel loneliness and depression by providing good companionship.*

Pets are not negative, contentious, or argumentative, they can't complain and they are content to live in the moment without regard to the past or the future.

4. ***Dwell on Solutions*** - *When faced with a problem, it is far more productive to concentrate your thinking on imagining solutions rather than continuing to focus on the problem itself and its troublesome effects.*

- *Use your energy and imagination to brainstorm a game plan for solving the problems.*

- *This also will break the **victim mentality**, which is a sure path to unhappiness. The victim mentality assumes that our problems and unhappiness are the result of others somehow holding us back or "the system" holding us down. Such an attitude is the source of many problems and much unhappiness.*

**There is no cure for either birth or death
except to enjoy the time between.**
...Philosopher George Santayana

5. ***Build Friendships*** - *Good friends contribute greatly to human happiness.*

- *Good friends are supportive of each other and not so competitive that they put one another down to make themselves look good.*

- *Having a good friend means being a good friend.*

- *Friendships require an investment of time with other people and a willingness to develop the interpersonal skills to relate well to them.*

- *Not only can good relationships with other people contribute to your happiness, but according to scientific research, they can also help you stay in good health and live longer.*[2]

6. ***Children and Grandchildren*** - *Human beings report that their children and grandchildren are often their greatest sources of happiness.*

7. **Laugh** - *Finding things to laugh about is a sure way to elevate joy.*

- *Laughter is contagious and good for your health.*

- *One study has shown that laughter increases blood flow by 27%, while stress decreases it by 35%.*[3]

- *Happy, hopeful, optimistic people are healthier in spirit, mind and body.*

8. ***Enjoy Comedy*** - *Watching, reading or listening to comedy helps establish an upbeat mood of joy. Appropriate kidding and joking around with friends, family and co-workers can help keep things from being too serious.*

- *Making jokes at one's own expense is much better than making jokes at the expense of others.*

- *"Laugh at yourself and the world laughs with you; laugh at others and the world laughs at you."*

It takes a long time to grow an old friend.
...Unknown

9. _Increase Pleasure_ - *Pleasure can be increased by slowing down enough to smell more of the roses along the path of life's journey and by concentrating on savoring and appreciating to a moderate degree more of the pleasure of life's sensory experiences.*

10. _Create Anticipation_ - *Having something to look forward to with positive anticipation contributes to happiness.*

- *Psychology and Neuroscience Professor Brian Knutson conducting studies to track happiness at Stanford University, found that the anticipation of a reward frequently creates greater happiness than actually receiving it.*

- *Having a vacation, trip or a party or anything big or small that is fun and exciting planned for some time in the near term helps establish a positive, eager sense about the future.*

11. _Enhance Happiness_ - *Dr. Clayton E. Tucker-Ladd notes the following four ways to enhance happiness:[4]*

- *Become able to manage your life doing **meaningful** things that **interest you**.*

- *Learn to feel truly **competent** in your major activities.*

- *Develop close, meaningful, mutually satisfying **relationships.***

- *Come to feel good about yourself and the life you have built for yourself.*

12. _Help Others_ - *Empathizing with the plight of other people and actively helping them with their problems is a sure path to human happiness.*

- *This strategy gets your mind off your own problems, which usually seem less imposing when compared to the problems of those who are less fortunate.*

- *Doing things to help other people gives more meaning and purpose to life because what you do matters to someone else.*

Problems and disappointments in life are inevitable, however, misery is optional.

- *In doing research for his book "Gross National Happiness,"[5] Professor Arthur C. Brooks found that people who give generously to help others are much happier than those who do not.*

- *Spending money on others makes us happier than spending it on ourselves according to Forbes Magazine.*

IV. More Ways to Become Happier

1. **_Be Optimistic_** - *Be a good finder who seeks to find the good in people and situations instead of being a faultfinder. The good finder brings goodness and happiness to the lives of others and happiness to their own lives in the process.[6]*

2. **_Avoid Negative People_** - *Recognize the importance of avoiding constant exposure to negative people and their sour attitudes. Professional gripers and constant complainers are never happy; they seldom have a good word to say about others, and they tend to want to spread their negativity to other people.*

3. **_Keep the News in Perspective_** - *Be wary of the news media with its 24-hour a day barrage of murder, mayhem, rape, disaster and scandal from around the globe.*

   - *Keep in mind that overall, things are not nearly as depressing as the news media suggests.*

   - *The news organizations are profit driven enterprises that profit the most by covering only what they can sensationalize and by sensationalizing whatever they cover.*

   - *Bad news sells, and the worse it sounds, the better it sells.*

4. **_Control Your Circumstances and Earn What You Get_** - *People are happier when they feel that they have some control over their lives and that they are carrying their own weight in society.*

> **"Most folks are about as happy**
> **as they make up their minds to be"**
> *...Abraham Lincoln*

*Every one percent increase in **economic freedom** leads to a two percent increase in the percentage of a country's population that reports themselves as being very happy according to an analysis of socio-economic policy in 35 countries cited in the Index of Economic Freedom by professor Arthur Brooks.*

5. **_Train Yourself to be Resilient_** - *People who are resilient are better able to bend and bounce back when hit with life's inevitable problems. According to Psychologist Martin Seligman, resilient people tend to be happier.[7] The following inner strengths add up to resilience:*

   - *Emotion Regulation*

   - *Impulse Control*

   - *Causal Analysis (understanding cause and effect)*

   - *Understanding and appreciating our own abilities and effectiveness*

   - *Realistic Optimism*

   - *Empathy (understanding and relating to another's feelings)*

6. **_Develop Confidence in Yourself_** - *Every human being has faults, weaknesses and limitations, and no one person knows everything or is expected to know everything. So, there is no reason to be defensive about your own deficiencies.*

   - *It is refreshing to be with people who are open to suggestions and ideas from others instead of acting as if they know it all.*

   - *Mature people know it doesn't diminish their own stature to acknowledge that someone else might know more about something or have a better idea.*

   - *Make a conscious effort to build a quiet, humble self-confidence and give yourself credit for your strengths. People are often their own worst critics, and that detracts from their happiness.*

- *Life is a learning experience, so learn as much as you can, and feel free to acknowledge that you don't know it all.*

- *At the same time identify your character weaknesses and work hard at making improvements.*

- *People who act like they know it all fool no one but themselves, because most people realize they are just covering up for their insecurity.*

It takes a much stronger person to accept criticism than it does to dish it out. Insecure people have great difficulty accepting criticism.

- *It also takes character strength to apologize sincerely when appropriate, instead of always insisting things aren't your fault.*

- *In both cases, the difference is a matter of self-confidence. Confident people are much happier than insecure people, so work on self-confidence.*

7. _Luck_ - *good luck and bad luck don't influence happiness for long. For example, big lottery winners after a few months are no happier than the average person! Luck is where preparation meets opportunity.*

"Life is really about creating meaning. And meaning does not come from what you get; it comes from what you give. It's who you become and what you contribute that will make you happiest."[8]
...Author Tony Robbins

V. Professional Tips for Being Happier

1. _Maintain a Healthy Life Style_ - *A healthy diet with adequate rest and exercise will combat stress, reduce sickness and disease and reduce the unhappiness that goes with them. Exercise helps keep your body in tone and boosts your spirit as well.*[9]

2. _Reframing_ - *Circumstances and issues that create unhappiness are often unavoidable; however, it is sometimes possible for humans to change their perspective on a situation in a way that considers potentially positive aspects that were previously overlooked.*

- *Looking at things in a "new light" or from a "different angle" can change one's reaction to an unavoidable situation.*

- *The technique of reframing requires a conscious effort, and it works best on life's many small inconveniences and normally bothersome problems.*

- *For instance, being stuck in a traffic jam normally elicits a negative reaction, but if it can't be avoided, it could be seen as an opportunity to think about things, listen to music or just relax instead of being tense and spending the whole-time fuming.*

3. _Span of Control_ - *The key to wisdom and happiness, according to the ancient Roman philosopher Epictetus, is to understand that we have complete control over only three things: our mind, our thoughts, and the actions we choose to take based on our thoughts.*

- *We do not even have complete control of our bodies, as they get sick, broken, old and dead.*

- *Short of mental health problems, you have complete control over what you think, and through that process, you can control your destiny.*

4. _Build Family Support_ - *A sense of belonging and social support can greatly increase levels of human happiness.*

- *Developing strong bonds with family members can provide the kind of support that sustains a greater level of satisfaction with life.*

- *However, it requires a willingness to provide support as well as a willingness to receive it.*

5. Music - *Listening to upbeat music is a great mood lifter.*

- *Many people listen to their favorite tunes as background music while doing other things.*

- *Young people often use music to offset the negativity and stress in their lives, but it works well for people of all ages.*

6. Seek Goodness, Truth and Unselfishness - *By actively seeking goodness and truth in your thought life, you will find wisdom and happiness and the bliss and peace thereof. Give up the lesser happiness of selfishness, and gain the greater happiness of generosity*

7. Predictability and Uncertainty - *A senior fellow at the Brookings Institution, Carol Graham, has been studying happiness around the world for over ten years and he reports that many of the same things tend to make people happy, despite cultural differences.*

- *As previously noted, a good marriage, good health and adequate material resources are among things that universally make people feel happier.*

- *He has also observed that people can remain happier with* **predictable** *difficulty as opposed to* **unexpected** *difficulty even if the former is more severe.*

- *Lessons show that, in terms of their happiness, most people can adapt to less income and less luxury, but they don't adapt so well to less* **certainty***.*

- *Finally, it seems that happier people everywhere can adapt to almost anything and remain happy, while unhappy people can seem to have everything and still be unhappy.*

"Don't let what you cannot do interfere with what you can do."
...Pro football Coach John Wooden

8. *Three Components of Happiness*

As a result of his research, Dr. Martin Seligman finds three routes to happiness: [10]

1. **Pleasure** (sensory enjoyment)

2. **Engagement** (the depth of involvement with one's family, work, romance or hobbies)

3. **Meaning** (using personal strengths to serve some larger end)

Of the three roads to happiness, pleasure is the least significant. Seligman insists, "This is newsworthy because so many people build their lives around pursuing pleasure. It turns out that engagement and meaning are much more important."

VI. Other Happiness Considerations

1. Religious Faith - Religious faith lifts the spirit. In his book "Gross National Happiness,"[11] Professor Brooks notes that religious people are happier than their secular counterparts.

- Scholarly studies have shown that people of faith tend to be less depressed, less anxious, and less suicidal than nonreligious people.

- In addition, they are usually better able to cope with such crises as illness, divorce and bereavement.

Studies have also shown that the more a believer in God incorporates religion into daily living---attending services, reading Scripture, praying---the better off he or she appears to be on both measures of happiness: the frequency of joy and positive emotions and the overall sense of settled satisfaction with life.

- Religious certainty (the sense of unshakeable faith in God and the truth of one's beliefs) is closely linked with the overall feelings of satisfaction in life.

- Attending worship services, on the other hand, has a stronger correlation to the positive emotions or feeling of joy at the time.

Religious adherents of all ages appear to benefit from religious practices: "A national study involving 3,300 adolescents found that teens who attend religious services, read their scriptures and pray, feel less sad or depressed, less alone, less misunderstood, less guilty and more cared for than their non-religious peers." [12]

Religion's benefits can be roughly divided into four areas:

- *Social support*

- *Spiritual support*

- *A greater sense of purpose and meaning in life*

- *Avoidance of risky and stressful behavior*

*Each of these benefits has been shown to help increase or sustain happiness in human beings. It's not just the good and positive things religion provides that help people, but it's also the **negative** and **harmful behaviors it teaches against**.*

- *The **"thou shalt nots"**—no adultery, no drugs, and so on—keep people from getting addicted or otherwise increasing their level of stress through harmful, dishonorable and selfish behavior.[13]*

- *Religion works on our souls, specifically on our thought processes to lift them to an elevated and purer condition of mind.*

- *Academic studies have also shown that human beings who believe in life after death are happier than those who do not.[14]*

2. Marriage *- Research suggests that married people are generally happier than those who are unmarried, divorced, separated or widowed.*

- *A close, lasting, caring relationship is for many a wellspring of happiness.*

- *A quarrelsome relationship, on the other hand, can be the cause of much lasting unhappiness.[15]*

> **"It is one of the most beautiful compensations in life that no man can sincerely try to help another without helping himself."**
> *...Author and poet Ralph Waldo Emerson*

Studies have found that people with the highest expectations for wedded bliss often set themselves up for the steepest declines in happiness.

- *In reality, happiness in marriage is partly a function of mutual communication and interpersonal skills, and the way spouses handle disagreement.*

- *Couples would be less disappointed and much happier in marriage if their expectations were more in line with their communication skills, interpersonal abilities and the realities of their relationship.*

Nevertheless, studies indicate that if two people are identical in every way other than their marriage status, the married one will be consistently 18 percent more likely than the single one to rate themselves as very happy.[16]

3. Age – *As previously noted, age can be a factor. Being younger may contribute to higher levels of daily joy and exuberance, but older people tend to have a greater sense of satisfaction with their lives.*

- *There appears to be a general correlation indicating that modern adult humans become a bit less happy per year as they get older up to about their mid-40s or 50s.*

- *After that, they tend to become happier with each passing year up until their health begins to fail.*

4. Intelligence - *Being more intelligent as measured by having a higher IQ does not, in and of itself, lead to more happiness. Although, to the extent that being smarter reduces the odds of living in poverty, it can contribute to happiness.*

5. Education - *Being better educated does not by itself lead to greater happiness, but to the extent that it reduces the odds of living in poverty, it also can contribute to happiness.*

6. Sunny Weather - *Sunnier weather has not been proven to keep people happier.*

VII. Happiest Company

In review, the following 10 thoughts on happiness are from the **Happiest** Company's website at **www.happiest.com.** [17]

1. **<u>Focus on, capture and appreciate small positive moments.</u>** Feeling and expressing gratitude does more than improve your mood. Grateful people seem to be healthier, more energetic, less stressed and anxious, and they seem to get better sleep.

2. **<u>Surround yourself with happier people.</u>** Researchers at Harvard and the University of San Diego[18] actually found that each additional happy person you have as a friend increases your probability of being happy by **about 9%.**

3. **<u>Do nice things for others.</u>** Research has shown that spending money on others and even doing small acts of kindness for other people increases our satisfaction in life.

4. **<u>Spend more time with family and friends</u>.** Limited social interaction can be twice as bad for your health as obesity or as harmful as smoking 15 cigarettes a day.

5. **<u>Spend money on experiences instead of things</u>.** When spending their money on experiences rather than objects, most people report feeling happier.

The world has no room for unhappy cowards.
We must all be ready somehow to toil, to suffer, and to die with courage.
Your cause is no less noble because no drum beats
when you go out to your daily battlefields,
and no crowds cheer your coming home
from your daily victory or defeat!
...Author R. L. Stevenson

6. **<u>Get moving.</u>** *Exercising for as little as 20 minutes releases endorphins in our brains making us feel better.*

7. **<u>Set goals and don't make them too easy</u>.** *Research shows that striving toward challenging goals can make people happier, suppress negative feelings and increase positive emotions.*

8. **<u>Get more sleep!</u>** *Research has shown that about 6-8 hours of sleep a night makes most people happiest.*

9. **<u>Try to learn new things.</u>** *People with a variety of experiences seem to be more positive.*

10. **<u>Living well and healthy</u>** *Being happier isn't just more fun; it's **important for living well** and staying **healthy**[19]*

   - *Thinking more positively has been shown to reduce significantly the chances of a heart attack, cold or even the flu.*

   - *You can reduce your risk of having a stroke or becoming depressed by being more optimistic.*

   - *Happier people live longer. According to psychological tests, pessimistic adults were shown to have higher death rates over a 30-year-period than optimists (optimists were more likely to take better care of themselves and be healthier).*

   - *A negative attitude can speed up aging because it causes stress and inflammation. This is likely why positive people live longer.*

**An Irish proverb notes, "A good laugh and a good night's sleep
are among the best cures in the doctor's book"**

VIII. Summary

- *Happiness is a most enjoyable state of the soul, yet it cannot long endure without occasional sadness or boredom to provide the perspective to make it so.*

- *Actively practicing religious faith and good marriages correlate with increased happiness as does exercise and upbeat music.*

- *Happiness is improved by living a healthy lifestyle, keeping a positive attitude and developing confidence and resilience.*

- *Strong family relationships, good friends, laughter, pets and positive experiences contribute much more to real happiness than owning more things.*

The Colonel does not share completely Carter's newfound conviction that happiness might be the preferred or natural state of the soul. However, he does agree that our souls are being shaped by the way we live, and living with more happiness should be a good thing.

Since Carter survived four tough years as an ascetic, his grandfather feels the young man deserves to see how happiness might affect his soul. It seems a worthwhile experiment and one that seems likely to increase their knowledge of the human soul.

However, the Colonel wants to look into some more research on happiness as it relates to work. Like all happiness, joy and satisfaction with work is largely within the power of the individual, but he knows there is more to learn about it.

Good family relationships promote happiness.

Results from Scientific Studies on Self-Control[20]

As previously noted, self-control is said to be the door to heaven; it has no substitute, and no power in the universe can establish it for us, and happier are they that can control themselves.

1. Studies show that average humans experience a 50% failure rate when attempting to exercise self-control over reasonable levels of temptation.

2. Human beings seem to have a finite amount of mental energy or willpower they can apply to restraint and self-control each day.

3. Self-control is twice as important as IQ as a predictor of success in human life. As they grew up, kids who tested best on their ability to delay gratification had the best success in life.

4. The ability to exercise will power or delayed gratification improves with age in both humans and animals.

5. The more we practice self-control the easier it gets to deploy will power sufficient to meet our needs.

6. Practicing self-control in one area of life can increase our ability to exercise will power and impulse control in other areas of life as well.

7. The consumption of alcohol or illegal drugs diminishes will power, self-control and restraint in human activity.

8. Modern culture requires more self-control for successful living than societies of previous eras.

9. Benjamin Franklin noted that, "By failing to prepare, you are preparing to fail."

**Pray not for fewer challenges,
but for more courage and determination.**

---

[1] Proceeding of the National Academy of Sciences, Dec. 4th 2012,

"Estimating the Influence of Life Satisfaction and Positive Affect on," Later Income Using Sibling Fixed Effects," by Jan-Emmanuel De Neve, and Andrew J. Oswald. © 2012 by the National Academy of Sciences. http://www.pnas.org/content/109/49/19953

[2] Research by Harvard Professor Robert Putman in the June 2006 issue of Trends Magazine – Marketing p. 1 of 4

[3] Time Magazine, December 2005, p 73.

[4] http://www.psychologicalselfhelp.org/Chapter6.pdf

[5] Prof. Arthur C. Brooks, *Gross National Happiness: Why Happiness Matters for America- and How We Can Get More of It*, published by Basic Books, Perseus Books Group, 2008. p.192

[6] Sermon by D. James Kennedy

[7] Research by Martin Seligman cited in the June 2006 issue of Trends Magazine – Marketing p. 1 of 4

[8] Tony Robbins, *Money Master the Game*; Simon & Schuster, NY; p.78

[9] Reader's Digest October 2012 reporting on University of Connecticut research.

[10] http://content.time.com/time/magazine/article/0,9171,1015832-3,00.html

[11] Arthur C. Brooks, *Gross National Happiness: Why Happiness Matters for America — and How We Can Get More of It*, published by Basic Books, a member of the Perseus Books Group, 2008.

[12] Pamela Paul, The Power to Uplift, Time Magazine, 17 Jan. 2005

[13] Dr. Harold Koenig, at the Center for Spirituality, Theology and Health at Duke University from 2000 to 2002

[14] Christopher Ellison, University of Texas at Austin

[15] Dr. Clayton E. Tucker-Ladd http://www.psychologicalselfhelp.org/Chapter6.pdf)

[16] Prof. Arthur C. Brooks, *Gross National Happiness: Why Happiness Matters and How We Can Get More of It*, Basic Books, Perseus Books Group, 2008, p. 30

[17] www.happiest.com – 02/26/14

[18] Dr. Nicholas Christakis et al

[19] http://www.huffingtonpost.com/david-r-hamilton-phd/positive-people-live-long_b_774648.html

[20] Professor C. Nathan DeWall, course 1637, *Scientific Secrets for Self-Control*, Chantilly, VA, The Great Courses, 2013

"Be the light for someone's darkness"
...Bob Welch

Chapter 5

<u>The Soul of Work and Happiness</u>

Carter's parents, Matt and Casey, visit Carter and the Colonel to relay a message from Warden warning Carter that APOLLYON has threatened both Warden and Doctor Moses. Warden, therefore, wants Carter to be extra careful. Carter's mom and dad ask what APOLLYON is and why they should want to hurt Warden. Carter explains what happened in the Athens Park and the message delivered to the Colonel's house via brick.

Some quick computer research on APOLLYON reveals that it is a radical, socialist, atheist organization known for trying to silence outspoken Christians. It also intimidates honest news reporters, government officials and judges in a major effort to discredit both religion and the free enterprise economic system (aka capitalism) in order to push the country into Socialism. It is even rumored that APOLLYON has threatened the family of a Supreme Court Justice to force him to vote their way on critical cases.

Matt and Casey return home concerned for the safety of Carter and Warden. Matt tells his wife that Carter is probably safer with the Colonel and his dog Chase than anywhere else. They both wonder though about Warden and the unusual doctor he is working for, and decide to keep Warden's folks informed about the situation.

In their research on happiness, Carter and his grandfather came across some very interesting data on happiness that related to success on the job. This was of special interest to the Colonel because he had a lot of experience working in all kinds of jobs where he observed some very positive productive employees and some that were very negative and unproductive.

Delving into one of his favorite subjects, Carter's grandfather, the old economics professor, explains to Carter that all improvements in human prosperity are based in one way or another on increased labor force productivity, which means finding ways to make more with less. This is done through human **effort** and **ingenuity** by discovering better tools like new machines, computers, or new software and with new businesses finding new products and smarter ways to do things.

Less motivated, less productive people, he says, are a drag on businesses, and together they add up to a drag on their communities and a drag on the nation's economy. The Socialism supported by APOLLYON creates less productive people because under communism and socialism the oppressive and counterproductive, principle of "equality of income" is more important than the principle of personal freedom and the equal opportunity for each individual to improve life via hard work, saving and investment or taking risks to start a business.

Therefore, if you study hard and put yourself through training to become an auto mechanic, a teacher or a doctor, under Socialism, you might be told it's not fair for you to make more money than another. To keep things equal, everyone makes the same minimum wage or your taxes are so high that you end up with about the same minimum amount after taxes. The same goes for your sister who borrows money and takes big risks to set up and start a business. Her profits are heavily taxed to keep her income down.

That may sound fair to some, says the Colonel, but the unfortunate result is that it causes people to be less willing to study long, work hard or take risks to improve their lives (and the economy) because the system is set up to keep them from getting ahead. Therefore, you eventually lose the desire to work hard and ultimately the whole society works less and less and starts fewer and fewer businesses resulting in fewer jobs and less tax revenue to the government.

Over the years, the Socialist and Communist countries become poorer and poorer and people become more dependent on government. Taxes are raised more and more to run a huge inefficient government. However, the people at the top running the government treat themselves very, very well, while everyone else suffers. Meanwhile, Capitalist countries continue to become more prosperous and their people enjoy better lives as the incentives of Capitalism continue to improve efficiency and productivity in those countries, said the professor.

We are adding over 75 million new people to the earth's human population each year, he said, at a rate of about 2 people per second. It's estimated that the world's growing population will consume well over **twice** the amount of food in this **century alone** than has been consumed in the **last 100 centuries combined**.

Some countries have over a billion people, and many of them are moving up from poverty to a more prosperous, middle class lifestyle, as their economies shift from socialism to capitalism. That means driving cars and owning nice homes, eating well etc. all of which will take a lot more resources per person than it did when they were poor.

We must constantly find smarter ways to do just about everything, just as we have been doing for centuries, with new technology and knowledge that keeps improving and providing new and better ways to get things done. To improve our living standards, we must be motivated to look constantly for more efficient ways to do our jobs. Capitalism provides the incentives to strengthen that motivation, but Socialism removes the incentives and weakens motivation.

The motivation to do our very best to be efficient and productive is now critical. Because, improving efficiency and productivity are the best ways to keep us from becoming poorer as the Earth's booming population requires more and more food, clothing and shelter plus all the other human needs of the 75 million additional people per year.

It is the duty of every citizen, he added, to keep our country free and prosperous by applying themselves to their work in the most dedicated, efficient manner possible so as not to be vanquished economically by those in other countries.

The Colonel wanted to be sure that Carter understood the importance of being a productive member of society. One of the best ways in life to serve unselfishly the needs of other people is by doing our part to help improve labor force productivity. This means doing our jobs to the very best of our abilities and constantly looking for better, more efficient ways to use resources and serve customers.

The Colonel and Carter's findings on happiness at work are presented on the following pages of the Handbook of the Soul.

Never expect your boss or another person to make you happy. Remember it is you and only you that can decide your level of happiness.

Handbook of the Soul

Secrets of the Soul and Happiness at Work

I. Preview

- *Happy people make much more valuable employees than unhappy people.*

- *You have to work hard at doing the right things to achieve happiness and job satisfaction.*

- *Research clearly shows that there are significant benefits to being happy at work. Among them are better performance reviews, faster promotion, higher income, better health, more energy and increased happiness with life.*

- *Working adults spend many of their waking hours at work, so happiness at work and job satisfaction can be a major contributor to your overall, settled feeling of satisfaction and happiness with life.*

II. Smile, it just might be a good career move!

*Experts say happy employees are more productive, earn more and are promoted faster! There are many factors involved in human happiness among which are job satisfaction and feelings of **meaning** and **purpose** in our work.*

- *Every job presents opportunities for commitment, meaning, engagement and purpose in trying to be the very best at what we do.*

- *We should be trying to overcome the challenges and difficulties of the job with a positive attitude, creative problem solving and productive teamwork in order to best serve our customers and keep our employers profitable and in business.*

Understood in this context, any job should be able to provide a measure of job satisfaction that contributes to your overall level of happiness. If not, look first within yourself at what you can control, namely your thoughts, your attitude and your actions.

*Then let your supervisor know that you are seeking more **engagement** and **satisfaction** from your work, to see if there are opportunities for cross training, temporary moves, skill training or paths to advancement where you work.*

**That every person may eat, drink, and find satisfaction in all his toil---
this is the gift of God.**
...Ecclesiastes 3:13

Jessica Pryce-Jones, *author of "**Happiness at Work**" and CEO of iOpener confirms once more that "Happiness at work is closely correlated with greater performance and productivity" as well as:*

- *Greater Energy*

- *Better Reviews*

- *Faster Promotion*

- *Higher Income*

- *Better Health*

- *Increased Happiness with Life*

Therefore, happiness at work is good for individuals, their employers and the nation.[1]

*1. **People at the Top** - Pryce-Jones also said people who are at the top of their organizations are about twenty percent happier in all her key indicators like goal achievement, resilience, motivation and confidence.*

*2. **Benefits of Happier Employees** - After conducting research with 3,000 respondents in 79 countries, Pryce-Jones established that happy people have a distinct advantage over unhappy people because the happiest employees are reportedly*

- *180 percent more energized than their less contented colleagues*

- *155 percent happier with their jobs*

- *150 percent happier with life*

- *108 percent more engaged in their work*

- *50 percent more motivated*

- *50 percent more productive*

*3. **Such productivity** is a boon, notes Pryce-Jones because*

- *The happiest employees reported focusing on what they are paid to do **80 percent** of their time at work.*

- *The least happy employees focused on what they were supposed to be doing only **40 percent** of the time.*

- *This means they are putting in only two days of real focused work a week, while their happiest colleagues are doing twice that much.*

- *It makes a difference of more than two days a week per person, so employers definitely **don't want unhappy workers** on their teams.*

__4. Sick Leave and Turnover__ – Trends Magazine research showed the least happy employees taking 66 percent more sick leave than those who are happy. Also, happier employees have been shown to stay with their employers longer resulting in less turnover.[2]

__5. Positive Energy__ - Ultimately a sense of happiness will boost your magnetism and increase the recognition you receive for your work, said Pryce-Jones adding:

- *"Who wants to work with a pessimist?"*

- *"Everyone is drawn to positive energy naturally, and that's because it's a secret indicator of success."*

__6. Increased Productivity__ - Pryce-Jones repeated that "People who are happiest at work have about 180 percent more energy than their least happy colleagues."

- *And that definitely translates into increased productivity.*

- *On the other hand, if you're unhappy, you'll be "less creative, less able to solve problems, and you're more likely to be spreading your misery as well."*

__7. Confirmation__ - Sonya Lyubomirsky, Ph.D., professor of psychology at the University of California, researched happiness and how it pays off with higher pay and promotions, showing positive outcomes when you're happier in the office.

- *She confirmed Pryce-Jones findings.*

- *According to her research, benefits of happiness include higher income and superior work outcomes (i.e., greater productivity and higher quality of work).*

8. _Emotional Contagion_ - *Gretchen Rubin, New York Times bestselling author of "The Happiness Project," refers to "emotional contagion" which is when people catch the happy, sad or angry moods of others.*

- *A happy employee will boost the mood of his or her colleagues, so it makes sense that "happy people are good for teams."*

- *This is "particularly important when that person is engaged with customers, clients, patients or a work team."*

9. _Unhappy, Apathetic and Detached_ - *The 2011 Gallup-Healthways Well-Being Index, which had been polling over 1,000 adults every day since January 2008, revealed the following:*

- *Employees felt worse about their jobs and work environments than ever before.*

- *People of all ages, and across income levels, seem to be more unhappy with their supervisors, more apathetic about their organizations and more detached from what they do.*

10. _Disengagement Crisis_ - *In a 2010 study, James K. Harter and colleagues confirmed that lower job satisfaction foreshadowed poorer bottom-line performance.*

- *Gallup estimates the cost the disengagement crisis at a staggering **$300 billion** in lost **productivity annually.***

- *When people don't care about their jobs or their employers, they don't show up consistently, they produce less, or their work quality suffers.*

III. Happier People Are More Productive

1. _Huge Part of Life_ - *A New York Times editorial offered insight on how important workplace happiness can be, not only for the individual* employees, but also for a company's overall productivity.[3] Work is a huge part of life because most of us do it daily.

2. _12,000 Diary Entries_ - Article authors and researchers Teresa Amabile and Steven Kramer collected 12,000 diary entries from almost 250 professionals. They found that many of their study's participants were unhappy or unmotivated at their jobs.[4]

3. _Creativity and Commitment_ - The authors found that employee's inner work lives -- their usually hidden perceptions, emotions and motivations--have a profound impact on their creativity, productivity, commitment and collegiality.

4. _Engaged Meaningful Work_ - When employees were engaged with meaningful work, they did their best work, and the feelings of accomplishment led to continued productivity. "Happy employees are far more likely to have new ideas and perform better," said Amabile and Kramer.

5. _Unhappy People Disengage_ - The authors also noted that unhappy people, who are disengaged from their work, don't generally care about their jobs or their employers.

6. _Progress in Meaningful Work_ - Of all the events that engage people at work, the single most important --- by far --- is simply making progress in work they consider meaningful. Progress in meaningful work is the primary motivator, well ahead of traditional incentives like raises and bonuses.

IV. Happier People Do Make Better Employees.

Economists also have confirmed a link between workers' happiness and their performance.

1. _Clear Links_ - A team of economists led by Andrew Oswald, a professor of economics at Warwick Business School, has conducted research that confirms clear links between workers' happiness and their productivity.[5]

2. _Positive and Negative Emotions_ - Oswald said, "We find that human happiness has large and positive causal effects on productivity."

The team noted, "Positive emotions appear to invigorate human beings, while negative emotions have the opposite effect."

3. _Twenty-Two Percentage Point Difference_ - The Warwick economists noted that happier workers were 12% **more** productive than normal, and unhappier workers were 10% **less** productive than normal for a total difference of about 22 percentage points.

The fact that we spend so many of our waking hours at work suggests that there is great opportunity for our work to contribute to, or detract from our overall level of joy and satisfaction with life.

- Very often, what makes the most difference in our **level of job satisfaction** is the **ways we respond** to the challenges of our jobs.

- Most of us need to feel that we are contributing in some way, perhaps by meeting goals or objectives on our jobs.

- Many jobs have numerical measures of the important results that we try to meet or exceed, and sales people usually have sales quotas to achieve.

- These measures can be a way of keeping score like a sports contest.

- People can help one another enjoy their jobs and their lives with the use of humor and wit.

Life is what we make it, and work is likewise, what we make it, so let's make sure we are using humor at work to contribute to our overall satisfaction with life. David Myers summarizes several of the very important ways to seek a happier life at work:[6]

1. **_Act like a happy person_** - Smile, greet people, be outgoing and optimistic, even if you are a little down. Acting sour and unhappy keeps you feeling that way.

2. **_Find respected work_** that uses your talents and challenges you to do your best!

The ultimate wealth is a life of engagement, meaning and fulfillment.

3. _Get some exercise_ – *Get at least a little exercise every day.*

4. _Attend to friends, loved ones_ *and the other people you are privileged to serve in this life.*

V. Conclusion

- *Happy people make employees that are more valuable. You have to work hard at doing the right things to achieve happiness and job satisfaction, but it is worth the effort.*

- *Research clearly shows that there are significant benefits to being happy at work, such as better performance reviews, faster promotion, higher income, better health, more energy and increased happiness with life.*

- *Working adults spend most waking hours at work, so happiness and job satisfaction can be a major contributor to your overall, settled feeling of satisfaction and happiness with life.*

- *It is very important that we be innovative, efficient and productive on the job in order to help pull millions of people out of poverty and to improve our own living standards.*

Don't expect your employer to make you happy, it's not his or her responsibility.

All work is a vocation, a calling, a source of meaning and identity. In having a purpose most people find comfort, fulfillment, challenge and creative expression.

The quality of the work we do is a reflection of the character of our being, and it is an important aspect of satisfaction in our lives. It deserves sufficient attention and care to warrant pride in its accomplishment.

Again, you and only you can decide whether or not to be happy at work. Don't just depend on the employer or your circumstances to make you happy.

Like the rest of our experience on earth, work is helping shape who we are becoming based on how honestly, unselfishly and productively we carry out our responsibilities. The integrity of our souls soars when we do excellent work and suffers when we don't. Is your output worthy of your time and commitment? Does it satisfy and ennoble your soul?

Carter and the Colonel have completed their research on human happiness, and Carter is ready to go forth and try capturing some of the happiness he has learned so much about. The Colonel does caution his grandson **not to go overboard** and not to forget the principles he was raised on such as moderation, honor, unselfishness and self-control.

Carter and his grandfather believe they now have the answers to the second great question of their spiritual quest.

ARE HUMAN BEINGS ETERNAL SOULS TRAPPED IN BODIES?

We are currently indeed eternal but flawed souls temporarily trapped in human bodies that have physical and mental limitations. These limitations and the need to feed and care for our bodies force us to interact with other people.

The inherent moral and ethical challenges of dealing with other people along with the other trials of life on Earth continuously test us revealing the flaws in our spiritual character.

Our challenge as souls is to work to reduce the flaws in our character by adopting good values and virtues while striving to exercise good moral and ethical conduct. Our spiritual weapons and powers can enable us to do so.

Life is about the choices we make in living that determine the character of our souls. We must learn to properly control what we can control through our choices and trust the rest to God, Who can make our best effort good enough if it is truly our best.

Chapter 5 The Soul of Work and Happiness

Souls are composed of faculties humans consider to be the spirit, the mind, the will and the emotions. Each faculty is composed of numerous similar capacities. Important properties and capacities of the spirit are consciousness, self-awareness, creativity, inspiration, intuition, insight, and conscience.

Happiness, a key capacity, is an important trait of mature spiritual character. It is the ability to remain relatively happy, joyful and positive in spite of life's challenges and difficulties.

Human consciousness arises from the interaction of our souls and the brains of our physical bodies at the quantum level. Human personality can be affected by damage to the brain where the interaction is rooted.

Carter figures APOLLYON is still after him. So, after saying goodbye to his parents and his grandparents and of course Chase, he awakens at 3:00 in the morning. He dresses for hiking, grabs a pack, walking staff and his journal and slips outside on a dark, moonless summer night to begin what he thinks will be a great adventure experiencing happiness.

The series **Living as a Modern Soul in a Human Body** continues in *Book 3 Human Spiritual Powers* where Carter unexpectedly discovers an ancient accounting of the awesome spiritual powers of the human soul.

Motivation gets you started.
Habit keeps you going.
...Jim Ryub

---

[1] Jessica Pryce-Jones author of *Happiness at work* and CEO of iOpener
[2] Trends Magazine issue 038, published June 15th 2006
[3] NY Times editorial September 3rd 2011 Teresa Amabile, Prof Harvard Business School and Steven Kramer independent researcher, authors of "The Progress Principle"
[4] Ibid www.nytimes.comSeptember 4th 2011
[5] Observer Guardian.co.uk, Saturday July 10th 2010 by Jamie Doward www.theguardian.com)

---

[6] David Myers (1993) (http://www.davidmyers.org/"
Other resources:
Psychology professors James McNulty of Ohio State and Benjamin Karney of the University of Florida as reported by Sora Song and Elizabeth Coady in the Science of Happiness, Time Magazine of January 17th 2005.
Billy Graham, *Nearing Home* (Nashville: Thomas Nelson, 2011)

**Luck is where opportunity meets preparation,
for opportunity is an impatient force that wastes no time
on the unprepared.**

HUMAN PROGRESS

Above is the famous artistic illustration of human progress featuring the huge winged gear of industry representing increased economic productivity accompanied by figures representing leadership, science, labor and medicine.

Author
James L. Cannon
Lt. Colonel U.S. Army (Ret.)

Mr. Cannon is a retired university vice president, a former economics professor and a former corporate manager.

Lt.Col. Cannon is a Vietnam War veteran, who has served in the U.S. Air Force and the U.S. Army. He was also an undercover intelligence operative and retired as a decorated Army Reserve Intelligence Officer with the Defense Intelligence Agency in Washington, D.C.

As a community leader, the author has been a successful small city mayor; a chamber of commerce president and has served on the governing boards of several public organizations.

The Colonel holds University of Virginia degrees in economics and foreign affairs; GTE marketing, management and technology degrees and is an honor graduate of the U.S. Army's Command and General Staff College and a graduate of the University of Kentucky College Business Management Institute.

The author is happily married with a beautiful wife, two children, two grandchildren, a dog and a small business. His interests include philosophy, metaphysics and economics.

The author may be contacted by email at soulsline9@gmail.com

www.ingramcontent.com/pod-product-compliance
Lightning Source LLC
Chambersburg PA
CBHW070224140626
46555CB00018B/1268